Martyrs

Brave Hearts Series #2

God Bless,

Kathryn Griffin Swegart

Kathryn Griffin Swegart

Copyright 2019 Kathryn Griffin Swegart OFS
ISBN Print 9781097783144
Cover art credit and illustration credit: John Folley
www.johnfolley.com

Artist's conception of Father Rale's cabin and
the church as it looked in the 1700's.

…inspired by the lives of Fr. Sebastian Rale, S.J. and the Wabanaki people

Father Sebastian Rale, S.J, lived among the Wabanakis of Maine from 1694-1724

Go therefore and make disciples of all nations, baptizing them in the name of the Father and of the Son and of the Holy Spirit.
Matthew 19:20

Historical Note

One of the bloodiest wars ever fought on American soil was King Philip's War (1675-78). The conflict derives its name from the son of a Wampanoag chief, Massasoit, who maintained friendly relations with the Mayflower pilgrims. Massasoit's son adopted the name King Philip in honor of those peaceful times. After the death of Massasoit, King Philip was not able to maintain an alliance with British colonists. After the execution of three Wampanoag braves, war began. New England turned into a battleground, pitting British colonists against the indigenous people. At that time, 70,000 people lived in New England. By war's end, 5,000 were dead-- a percentage twice as deadly as the Civil War and seven times greater than the American Revolution. It was a time of high mortality rates and intolerable cruelty. In 1678, King Philip's War came to an end, but in reality, it was only the beginning of a series of wars between the British, French, and indigenous people.

Tensions mounted between French and British settlements in North America, fueled by lack of clear boundaries and religious differences. With the capture and killing of King Philip, the battleground shifted north to the wilderness of Maine. Scattered British settlements were vulnerable targets for raids by local tribes. Some of the bloodiest attacks of these

New England conflicts were on the coast of Maine. As British farmers tilled the rocky soil, fear was a constant companion. They nervously stared into the dark pine forests, believing every movement could mean an attack. Pamphlets arrived from Boston stating that French Canadians instigated local tribes to kill settlers and burn down villages. According to these pamphlets, the worst troublemakers were Jesuit missionaries who lived among the indigenous people.

In every war there must be a lightning rod for hatred. That enemy must be evil personified. As British propaganda pamphlets were printed and distributed to colonists, one name stood out above all the rest. Father Sebastian Rale, S.J., was a missionary living with the Wabanaki people in Norridgewock, along the banks of the Kennebec River. British leaders saw him as a man in league with the devil. Soon after Father Rale arrived in the New World, Jesuits were banned from the colonies. No one could have imagined that this refined Jesuit, trained in the finest universities in France, could live among the Wabanakis for thirty years. Meanwhile, hatred for Father Rale and racial bigotry toward the indigenous people boiled over in the year 1724. A price was put on Father Sebastian Rale's head; the British sharpened their knives and took to the woods, intent on scalping his gray head. After thirty years of this Frenchman living among the Wabanakis, the time had come to take his scalp.

Chapter 1

Dark Forces

It was his stride that told the story. Father Sebastian Rale did not stroll or meander. His stride was bold and full of purpose. Strong it was, from a childhood climbing the hills near the border of France and Switzerland. Strong it was, on the day in his eighteenth year, when he stepped up to the wooden door at the Jesuit seminary in Dole, France. The year was 1670. As the door closed, leaving behind his family, Rale never looked back; he always turned inward, listening to a voice, supernatural in origin. God called him to be a priest …to be a Jesuit priest …to be a missionary to the indigenous people of the New World.

In the year 1689, after years of study and teaching, Father Sebastian Rale strode up the gangplank to board a sailing ship bound for Quebec, Canada. It was not a ship to inspire confidence. Barnacles and seaweed clung to her hull, weather-beaten from many harrowing passages across the Atlantic Ocean. Provisions were stored in the bottom hold; passengers lived in a dark, stuffy crawlspace below the upper deck.

People crowded together—women and children, farmers and tradesmen—all making the perilous voyage to start a new life across the ocean.

Ten weeks into their three-month voyage, Father Rale paced the deck, staring intently at the sky. Trouble was brewing, of that he was certain. He grabbed hold of the mast and climbed briskly to a vantage point with a clear view. Clouds shaped like mares' tails spread across the sky. No longer was the sun bright against a blue sky. Instead a ring circled the sun. No longer did the ocean roll in soft rhythms. As far as the eye could see, the agitated surface was white and bubbly. A brisk wind chilled him to the bone. Something churned in the pit of his stomach. Black clouds loomed overhead, and the water looked wild, whipped into chaotic peaks of white foam. Suddenly, the ocean took on a new form. It seemed alive to him, like an evil force in search of prey. Out of the depths rose a gigantic wave, bearing down on the ship. In the shadow of that wave, God spoke to him. You will reach land and enter into a wilderness. Other dark forces, evil beyond imagination, await your arrival, fully intending to kill you in a most brutal fashion. Prepare for spiritual battle.

Soon after his arrival in the New World, Father Rale visited the St. Lawrence River, a long river that cuts through Quebec. He had never seen a river like this before, swift with whirlpools of icy water. The St. Lawrence River rushed below the city of Quebec, down from Lake Ontario into the Atlantic Ocean. On this early spring day of 1690, the Jesuit prepared to navigate a canoe in rushing waters; thunder from the river filled the air. Waters streamed over boulders that lay on the pebbly soil below. Father Rale listened to the roar and knew death awaited all who fell overboard. A shudder rippled over his flesh. His companions were two native men from the village of St. Francis de Sales. Father Rale lived in wigwams, sat next to smoky campfires and learned their language.

As they prepared to launch, he surveyed the thin birch-bark sides of the canoe, no match for jagged ice floes rippling down the St. Lawrence. One thing was on his mind: a sick baby lay dying in a wigwam across the river. He prayed, Dear Lord, bring us safely across this river so that I might baptize your little one. Father Rale pulled up his black robes and climbed aboard with his companions. All he could do was trust that God would protect them. Immediately, he realized they were no match for the strong currents. Any attempt to steer the canoe was futile, as it was tossed about like a toy. In no time, a large ice chunk raced toward them and crashed into the bow; icy water flowed through the hole. Gigantic wedges of ice surrounded them, leaving no chance of escape.

One of the scouts shouted, "We are dead men, it is all over

for us, we must perish here!"

In this desperate moment, there was no time to think. "Trust God and follow me!" Father Rale shouted above the howling wind.

He plunged his paddle into the river over and over, struggling against the current. An enormous block of ice floated toward them. Just then an inner voice said, Head to the big ice and climb onto it. Father Rale paddled even harder until they bumped into the sharp edges of the ice.

"Jump onto it!" he yelled.

In unison, they sprang onto the slippery surface. "Now pull up the canoe!" Father Rale pulled with all his might, but the canoe slipped back into the river. His hands were numb with cold.

"Pull harder!"

Father Rale thought his arms would collapse, but still he held on, encouraging his friends. "Don't give up!"

They did not quit. They yanked and hauled until the canoe tipped onto the ice. Now a plan formed in his frozen brain. Straight ahead large ice chunks lined up in a row like a stone path—their escape route!

"See those ice chunks?" he pointed ahead. "Drop the boat into the water and head in that direction. It will take us to shore."

With total trust, the scouts did just that. Slowly they crept to the icy edge and slid their damaged canoe back into the river. Once again, they climbed aboard and paddled to the next floe, scrambled up, dragged the canoe with them, pushed it off and drifted ever closer to the riverbank. In this way, they jumped from floe to floe until finally they touched land, dripping wet and frozen to the bone.

Now he turned to his companions. "Lead me to the wigwam of the dying child."

One of them pointed to smoke rising from a nearby clearing. Father Rale slung a leather bag over his shoulder and was relieved that his bottles of holy water and sacred oil had not broken in the crush of ice. Together, the three men hiked through snow until they reached their destination. He raised the flap that enclosed the wigwam and was greeted by a woman cradling a crying infant, her face wet with tears. In the dim light of that tent, Father Rale looked into the woman's eyes and saw a spark of hope. As he opened his leather pouch, the priest whispered a prayer of thanks that God had brought him safely to this place, to this child.

~~~~

Father Rale spent two years with the Wabanakis at the Canadian village. Here he learned their language, ate their food, and was taught how to build a campfire. In 1689, he was ready to journey to his permanent assignment among the Wabanakis in a village located in what is now the state of Maine. One mighty river cut through the wilderness of an evergreen forest. Known as the Kennebec River, it flowed from the cold waters of Moosehead Lake to the north all the way south to the Atlantic Ocean. Father Rale dipped his paddle into the rippling stream. Dark green fir trees reflected in clear waters, springs bubbled up from leafy river beds. Silence reigned in these forests, broken only by the thunder of a distant waterfall and the call of woodland birds.

With sturdy hands, Father Rale paddled into this wilderness guided by scouts from Norridgewock village. The priest was dressed in black robes and a broad-brimmed hat. In his pack were prayer books, rosaries—his weapons of war. He was a young man, only 37, and strong with brown hair and a short beard to match. Father Rale was filled with enthusiasm; plans buzzed in his head. At first, he would place the altar stone—a granite slab that served as a portable altar— on a tree stump and say Mass under a canopy of trees. Later he would build a chapel. Around the bend was a clearing next to the riverbank. They had arrived at their destination. They skillfully slid the boat to shore, and the priest stepped onto a dirt path leading to Norridgewock village.

As he observed the sights and sounds around him, his heart

pounded with excitement. By the Wabanaki calendar, April was known as the moon in which to sow corn. Up in the fields, women carried bags of corn seeds, planting row after row. In a nearby tributary, alewives migrated upstream, choking the waters with thousands of fish. Smoke rose from the center of wigwams. Father Rale was far removed from France, from the university where he studied languages, philosophy, and theology, but in his heart, he was home. Home was the wilderness of Maine, where God had called him. For the people of Norridgewock village, Father Rale was a welcome sight. It had been more than thirty years since a priest had lived with them. Five times, Wabanaki leaders voyaged up to Canada to meet with the Jesuits to request a priest. In that time many babies had been born and not baptized. Many old people had died without the Last Rites. During all those years, none had received the Blessed Sacrament—the body and blood of Christ hidden under the appearance of bread.

As Father Rale walked up to the village, he gazed across a valley. Spring had come. Gray clouds piled up in the late afternoon sky, but soon rays of sun broke through the cloud cover, deepening the sky to a brilliant yellow haze. Warmer temperatures had softened the fields to a dark brown. Fir trees shone in blue-black colors. Mountain crests gleamed in a golden luster; in that sunlight, children played blind man's bluff. Among those who played was a seven-year-old girl with braids the color of night skies. She was named One-Who-Picks-Lilies, but everyone called her Lily. She was a slim, small-boned child with large dark eyes and long eyelashes. On this bright spring day, Lily ran so fast and so free it looked like she could fly; her father watched and smiled.

Lily's father was Chief Bomazeen, leader of the Wabanaki people. He stood six feet tall with broad shoulders and arms strong from a lifetime of hunting wild animals and paddling canoes through the churning white waters of the Kennebec River. Bomazeen was swift of foot. In winter snows, he strapped on snowshoes and could run down a deer. As Bomazeen watched the children play, he heard someone call his name. It was his son Mattawa, ten years old, a boy tall and muscular for his age. He looked like his father, but was of a different, more cheerful spirit, not weighed down with the worries of war and survival.

"Black Robe is here. Look! Over there! He walks up the hill," Mattawa called with excitement in his voice.

Many winters had passed since they had requested a priest. Bomazeen greeted the priest. "Welcome Father Rale!"

Father Rale interrupted. "You may call me Pere Rale."

Bomazeen nodded out of respect. "I journeyed up to Canada

to ask the Black Robes to send us a priest. Now the Great Spirit has answered our prayers. For that we are grateful. You come at a time of danger to my people. English settlers take over our lands and attack our villages. They lie to us and break treaties. They kill women and children. They take some of my people as hostages. We fight back. I do not want war. I want my village, my children, to live in peace."

Father Rale listened carefully. The priest shook hands with Bomazeen and said, "I have come to live among you and to teach you that the Great Spirit came down to earth as man. I come to teach you about Jesus Christ and his merciful love," said Father Rale. "I will stand with you against the English and tell of any lies they write in their treaties with your people."

At these words, Bomazeen took off a strip of red cloth he wore around his head. "We trade beaver fur for English goods, like this cloth. Many winters ago, before English settlers came, all our clothes were made of deerskin. Now we trade fur for tools, for hatchets and knives. Look at the women cooking with iron kettles. No longer do they cook in earthen pots." Silent now, Bomazeen stuffed the cloth in his pocket and called to his daughter. "Lily, come and meet the Black Robe!"

Lily stopped playing and ran to her father. Shyly, she stared at her feet. The priest reached into his bag and pulled out a small cross. "This is a gift for you. It reminds us of how the Great Spirit and His Son love us. Many years ago, a priest built a chapel here. Can you show me that chapel?"

In the center of the village stood a small hut built of tree branches and covered with birch bark. It was on that spot that Jesuit Father Gabriel Druillettes first constructed a chapel and said Mass. Father Rale knew well the hardships of this Jesuit. At the time of his mission, Father Druillettes was an old man with failing eyesight. Hunger and exhaustion took its toll, forcing the elderly priest to return to Canada. On the canoe trip back to Quebec, Druillettes and his guides ran out of food. Faced with starvation, they boiled down moose skin robes for sustenance.

Lily glanced up at the priest, wondering what he would say. Father Rale had a gentle manner and a kind voice, so different from gruff English traders. His brown eyes had a shining quality to them. He seemed to carry a secret joy. The priest smiled as he watched the girl study his black robe—a sight that must have looked strange to her. It was made of rough cloth and covered his whole body, falling as a skirt down to his ankles. Rale knelt and pulled a bottle of holy water from his pocket, making the sign of the cross in the dirt.

He prayed, "I bless this ground and pray that God guide us

that we may build a church to give glory to your name. We ask this in the name of Jesus Christ. Amen."

As he prayed, Lily fixed her eyes on the metal crucifix hanging from his neck. She squeezed the cross he had given her and slowly backed away, eager to play with her friends.

Chapter 2

Medicine Man

Now the northern woods were filled with the sounds of ax upon tree and hammer upon nail as Father Rale worked side by side with the men as they built a church. It was made of logs with windows all around and a steeple topped with a cross. Day by day they labored. Soon an altar was built, adorned with ornaments and sacred vessels. Women of the village brought him baskets and colored cloth. One thing was missing. Candles were needed on the altar for Mass and evening prayer, called vespers. It was not possible to receive a steady supply from his superior in Canada, nor could he ask the Wabanakis, for they had never seen lit candles.

Dear God, you know of our need for candles at Holy Mass, so please show me the way, he prayed. Not too long after saying this prayer, he noticed Lily making a crown for herself. It was made of white feathers, daisies, and tiny branches with pale green berries.

Father Rale smiled. "You will look like a little princess. What are those berries? I have not seen any in these woods."

Lily answered in a quiet voice. "My father brings them from the coast every year. After a day of fishing, he walks the shore and collects them for me. The smell of these berries makes me happy. It is the most beautiful smell on earth."

She reached into her basket filled with berries and gave a handful to the priest. He split one open and inhaled. Sure enough, it had a heavenly fragrance. On closer examination, he noticed that they were waxy, like candles. That got Father Rale thinking, and, as always, holy thoughts turned to holy actions.

"Lily, could I have some of these berries? I have an idea."

"Yes, Pere Rale," she said and gave him her basket.

"May I speak with your mother?" he asked.

Running Deer, Lily's mother, looked like her name. Slight of build, but strong and sleek, she was a leader among the other women. It seemed that she never stopped working to make the village a peaceful place. She often stood at a large kettle cooking food and singing songs about birds in the air or fish in the river. Always, women called to her for help in childbirth. Father Rale approached her with a question.

"May I use your pot?" he asked. Now this appeared to be a surprise to her because men of the village did not cook. Running Deer hesitated for a moment, but then said, "I will get water from the stream."

Father Rale threw wood onto the outdoor fire pit and placed a kettle over the flames. Soon water bubbled up and he dumped in the berries. Minutes later, oil covered the surface and he skimmed it off the top and put in a bowl. When the oil cooled, it hardened into a wax, but one too soft for candles. After more attempts, he mixed the soft wax with moose fat, making it as solid as any votive candle used in France.

"Voilà! We have real candles for our new church," Father Rale announced happily to the women. "Come to evening vespers and I will have a surprise for you."

As the last glimmer of sunlight sank below tall pine trees, the people left their wigwams and gathered outside the church. Father Rale stood at the entrance. In solemn procession, they entered the church. Lily held her mother's hand and stared in wonder. Twinkling candles lit the darkness like bright spirits dancing in the night. Flickering light shone on the faces of the people as they listened in silence to the prayer.

In a voice filled with joy, the priest prayed, "Lord Jesus, light in our darkness, peace in our storms, protection against all that frightens us, calm our hearts, that we may rest in peace in Your presence throughout this night, who live and reign with the Father in the unity of the Holy Spirit, one God forever and ever. Amen."

~~~~

One man lurked in a dark corner of the church. A pouch on his leather belt held a hunting knife. Silently, he took out the knife and felt its sharp edge. He was Gray Wolf, the medicine man, a person of great importance to the Norridgewock people for he gave out potions to the sick and could see into the future. As he watched this Black Robe, he leaned against the wall and stabbed a log, making a deep gash in the wood. He did not trust this white man who poisoned their minds with teachings about a strange god. One night he had a dream of English soldiers stalking their village and killing their people, including the priest. It was a dream so real that he sat up covered in cold sweat. Deep in the woods surrounding the village he heard Kokokhas, great horned owl and guardian of the Wabanakis, call out a warning. Gray Wolf must go talk to another bird, more powerful than Kokokhas. He must talk to First Bird, the pileated woodpecker, powerful animal spirit who was there at the dawn of time.

The next day, Gray Wolf disappeared into the deep forest searching for a dead tree. High overhead, trees swayed in the breeze, and crowns of beech and maple danced in the sunlight. He came to a dead pine tree stripped of its bark with large oval holes in the trunk, a sure sign that First Bird, named May-May, was near. Gray Wolf sat on the forest floor and remembered the last time he had talked with May-May.

Two winters ago, his son, Swift Arrow, had begged him to join in a raid against the English. Only twelve years old, he was swift of foot, eager for adventure. Gray Wolf did not talk to May-May about this. Instead, he agreed to let him come on a raid. In this fight, Swift Arrow was killed by gunfire.

Gray Wolf covered himself with pine boughs and whacked on the hollow tree with his knife. Kik-kik-kik-kik-kik, the bird answered. It flew, dipped and rose in flight, landing on the dead trunk next to Gray Wolf. May-May was large, with black feathers and a red crest on his head. A white stripe started at his neck and curved to his powerful beak. He hammered on the tree. Gray Wolf saw its barbed tongue search for food; watched as he stabbed at insects hidden inside the trunk and heard him crunch on ants.

Still hidden in the pine boughs, Gray Wolf whispered, "Great spirit bird of the Wabanakis, you breathed air into the First Man, taught us how to speak, taught us how to hunt. I need your help. My son Swift Arrow is dead. My heart is hollow, filled with holes, like this dead tree. His mother, Shining Star, also has a hollow heart. She blames me for his death. If only I had protected him … How can we live again? Tell me what to do."

May-May did not stop hammering on the tree, for that was

his way in the forest. Only by flying, drilling, and eating did he survive. Still, his spirit spoke from heart to heart. Go to war again. Look for a white boy. Capture him and take him back to the village. Teach him our ways. Make him your son.

Chapter 3

White Captive

One hot summer day, Mattawa and his friend Red Hawk retreated to shady paths in the woods. Red Hawk was ten years old, son of a brave who died in an attack on York village. Despite this tragedy, Red Hawk still found delight tramping through the forest with Mattawa. Many in the village thought that one day he would be chief. His spirit was strong as an oak tree, his black eyes alert for the slightest movement of the white-tailed deer. On the day Red Hawk's father did not return, he crouched at the riverbank and let his long hair fall over his face, hiding his tears. Mattawa sat next to him but said nothing.

Two years had passed since Red Hawk lost his father. Over that time, he grew stronger in spirit, seeking solace in his friendship with Mattawa. On this summer day, they headed for the river. Despite the forest shade, it was a sultry day, even next to the river. Red Hawk splashed water on his face. "We should go swimming. I wish Lily was here with us."

"The women were busy in the village. She had to help mother with the cooking," It was the first time Red Hawk had ever mentioned Lily. Mattawa thought it a curious thing to say, but he shrugged it off.

Here at a bend, water flowed over smooth rocks that covered the riverbed. A sharp crook in the river created a pool, deep and green. They ran down a hill toward the stream and leaped off the bank, cutting through the surface and diving under water. White perch scattered, and frogs kicked to shore hiding between boulders lining the shore. Side by side the boys swam underwater, submerged in a fluid world of light and dark, of sunbeams piercing the surface, of blackness deep below. They touched bottom, turned and catapulted themselves off the muddy bottom and into sunlight. Still dripping wet, they climbed on a flat granite boulder, warm with the sun. Birds of the deep forest called them. Upstream, Mattawa heard the thunder of a waterfall. Mingled with that sound came yelling, fierce and triumphant. Startled, he lifted his head and listened intently.

"Did you hear that?" he asked.

Red Hawk nodded. "Those must be the shouts of returning warriors who raided white settlements. I heard our braves talk by the fire. White men are coming ever closer to our lands, building forts and clearing forests for wood. Gray Wolf stirred up hatred in their hearts."

"I heard that too. Let's go."

As they splashed along the river's edge, racing downstream, shouts grew louder. At the shore near their village, dozens of canoes pulled up. Each canoe was filled with rifles taken in the raid. Gray Wolf stood by one canoe, eager to show off his greatest prize. A young white boy, barely nine years old, sat alone in the boat. His clothes were torn and splattered with blood.

"Our captive is strong and bold. He will make a powerful brave in our tribe. He will help me hunt and fish. I will make him my own son," Gray Wolf announced and lifted the boy onto shore.

Mattawa watched as warriors shoved the boy up to the campfire where women were boiling meat. The boy stopped and refused to move. Gray Wolf placed his foot on the child's back and knocked him to the ground. He lay there motionless, covered in dirt. Mattawa knew that Father Rale would not be pleased. Before every raid on British settlements, the Black Robe gave warning. Captives must not be treated with cruelty.

"Pere Rale will speak to Gray Wolf, of that I am sure," Mattawa said.

"It is the way of returning warriors. They will not listen," Red Hawk said.

Indeed, Father Rale did watch the scene unfold and walked swiftly over to the medicine man.

"Do not treat him that way!"

Gray Wolf ignored these words. He spoke with confidence. "He will be my son. His name will be White Feather. I must teach him to be tough, like me. I will prepare a bear mat for him. You tell him that he is now my son. He will learn our ways and help provide food and protection for our people."

"It is too soon after the raid to tell him this news. I am the only one who speaks his language. He needs to talk to a white man like me. For now, let me care for him."

Gray Wolf picked up an armful of flintlock rifles and turned toward his wigwam. "I will allow this for only a short time."

Mattawa stood a short distance away and observed the scene, wondering how the priest would respond. Father Rale helped the captive to his feet.

"What is your name?" he asked in English.

"I am Jeremiah Smith. Do not touch me," he said and wrenched his arm away. Father Rale studied the boy's face; even for the priest, it was strange to see a white face covered in freckles. Jeremiah's hair was rusty red and curly.

"Do you have a family?"

"My father fished off the coast. When the Indians attacked, he was out in his boat and did not see my mother killed and my house burned to the ground."

"I am a priest and will be sure that you are treated with kindness."

"I do not want your kindness. I will escape and go back to my father."

Father Rale ignored his words and handed him a bowl of stew. It contained bear meat, greasy and tough to chew.

Jeremiah spit it on the ground. "I'll never eat Indian food and I will not live with them."

Father Rale beckoned Mattawa. It was obvious that Jeremiah had to be separated from the men who killed his mother. The sight of warriors fueled his anger.

"Mattawa, take the boy into the woods for now, away from the village," the priest said. Father Rale had a strong sense that White Feather was prepared to cause great trouble in the village.

~~~~

Reluctantly, Jeremiah—now called White Feather—followed Red Hawk and Mattawa into the forest. Once out of sight of the village, the captive once again refused to budge. He stood in the path, clenching and unclenching his fists, glaring at Mattawa. In full leap, White Feather sprang on Mattawa like a wild animal, landing a punch to his ribs. Breath expelled from his stomach and Mattawa doubled over in pain. White Feather ran at him again. This time Mattawa blocked his punches and grabbed White Feather by the neck, holding him in a tight headlock. The boy struggled to free himself, kicking and elbowing, refusing to give up. Mattawa squeezed harder until he felt White Feather's body weaken and slump to the ground. Mattawa sat on top of him and pinned his arms to the dirt.

"Let me go!" White Feather screamed in English. Mattawa did not understand the words but knew what he said. It was clear that this boy would never accept their way of life. He had seen white captives before. The Wabanaki tribe adopted them, treating them like sons and daughters. All were expected to work in support of the people. Not this one. He would have to tell Father Rale. Mattawa returned to the village but could not find the priest and sought out his mother. Running Deer saw her son burst out of the forest; she paused from the work of hanging fish on a drying rack. Mattawa ran to her.

"Where is Pere Rale?" he asked.

"He is in the wigwam of old Earth Mother. She is dying."

Mattawa raced over and stood outside the tent, listening to the priest speak in quiet tones to the old woman. Earth Mother had many daughters who crowded into the wigwam. Mattawa peeked inside. Earth Mother was someone he always avoided, knowing that she would grab him by the shoulder and thrust a bucket in his hands, telling him to get water from the stream. Whenever the Black Robe came near, she turned her back and walked away. Now she was dying. Pus oozed out of a deep gash on her swollen arm — so bloated it appeared ready to burst.

It was strange to see Pere Rale at her deathbed. Mattawa saw a bottle of holy water used for baptism. It appeared that the old woman had been … he shook his head in amazement … it appeared that she had been baptized.

Father Rale bent over the woman, dipped his thumb into a bottle of blessed oil, and made the sign of the cross on her forehead.

"It will not be long now," he said. Her eyes were dull and glistening; white streaks stretched down from the corners of her mouth. It was the mark of death. Silently, they all waited, the priest with his head bowed. Earth Mother opened her eyes, taking in the sight of a white man praying for her. A change came in that moment; her eyes rolled up under the lids and a rattling sound came to her throat. Finally, her chest stopped moving and she breathed her last. As the daughters wept, Father Rale quietly left the tent and saw Mattawa waiting for him.

Mattawa told his story in anxious tones. "What should we do?" the boy asked.

"Watch over him. If he tries to run away, follow him."

For three days, White Feather refused to eat their food. Every day he sneaked away from the village and hid in the woods, eating wild mushrooms and drinking from the stream. Sharp rocks shredded his shoes until he was forced to walk barefoot. White Feather did not know that someone followed him. Mattawa hid behind fir trees, thick with balsam boughs, watching and waiting, unsure of how he could help. On the fourth day, White Feather waded along the riverbank and sat on rocks to check his bleeding feet. Suddenly, a large black snake slithered between the boulders toward White Feather. Mattawa spotted ripples in the water and knew what was happening. Hidden in the rocks was a nest of young snakes coiled in the water only inches from the boy. Without warning the adult snake lunged at White Feather and bit him in the leg. Blood flowed out of a gaping wound in his shin. The snake struck again, biting him in the heel. White Feather rolled away into a thicket of blackberry bushes filled with long thorns, scratching him in the face. For the first time since his arrival in the village, White Feather cried.

Mattawa knew the time had come. He ran to the thicket and squatted next to White Feather holding out his hand, watching as the captive wiped tears away. Moose flies buzzed around his head; black flies bit his neck; blood poured out of the snake bite. White Feather grasped Mattawa's hand and stood up.

"I will take you to Pere Rale," Mattawa said. White Feather did not understand the strange words, but this time, he did not fight.

To Mattawa's amazement, Father Rale acted like he expected their arrival. "Bring him into my cabin. I will bind his wounds. Mattawa, bring me a bowl of warm water."

Blood seeped out where the fangs had sunk deeply into his skin. Gently, the priest wiped dirt and blood from both wounds. When Mattawa returned with water, Rale drenched the bites with water, revealing clean punctures. Mattawa watched in silence. As the priest bent over to examine the leg more carefully, White Feather kicked the bowl, spilling it on the black robe.

"You must trust me," Father Rale said

"I trust no white man who lives with these savages." Every word flashed with anger.

"I am deeply sorry for the attack on your settlement," the priest said and then paused to think. "I have clothes for you to wear." He gestured toward a pile of clothes made of deerskin: a long shirt and broadcloth leggings embroidered with colorful beads.

"I will not wear that clothing," he said defiantly.

Father Rale showed him rugged moccasins made of moose

hide. "If you don't wear good shoes, you cannot escape through the woods."

White Feather said nothing but grabbed the moccasins and clothes.

Father Rale spoke to him softly. "Now hear my promise. I will do everything in my power to return you to your people."

Chapter 4
Danger

Now the nights were cool as autumn spread over Norridgewock village. Crickets sang in the grass and geese honked overhead, flying south in formation. After a rainfall, the strong smell of leaves filled the air. Each change of season meant new work for the tribe. For Lily and Mattawa, it was time to gather nuts in the forest.

"I will bring my bow and arrow," Mattawa said. He looped the bow around his shoulder and carried arrows in a shoulder bag.

"You will shoot a squirrel, oh, great hunter," Lily teased.

"Someday I will kill a deer and then you will not laugh. Watch me hit that tree," he said.

Mattawa whipped out an arrow and slid it onto the bow string. His father, Bomazeen, had shown him many times to pull the string back, focus on your target, and let go. Every arrow his father shot was straight and true. One day Mattawa was out hunting with his father in the silent woods. Bomazeen sensed movement, for a deer hid in a thicket. In one quick motion Bomazeen aimed the arrow and fired into the heart of a leaping deer.

"Put down your bow. We do not need food today," Lily said. "Our father has returned from fishing by the seas. We have cod and clams. Let our friends – all deer, moose, elk – let them live until we are hungry in winter." She squinted at towering pines and listened to the swish of wind through the pine needles. Acorns, beechnuts, chestnuts lay strewn the forest floor, food to gather in abundance.

Mattawa stood guard over his sister. An uneasy feeling had settled in his stomach. Something was not right. He heard branches cracking on the forest floor. Was someone watching them? Now Lily was pretending to make acorn soup, stirred the brown seeds with an invisible spoon. That's when it happened. A figure bolted out of the shadows straight at a large dead tree and pushed hard. The tree teetered and tipped toward Lily.

"Watch out!" Mattawa cried, running toward her. He scooped up his sister and they both fell just as the tree crashed to the ground, inches from their feet. Mattawa's face hit a rock and began to bleed. As they lay on the forest floor, Lily began to cry.

"Why did the tree fall?" she whimpered.

"Someone pushed it."

"Who would try to hurt us?"

Mattawa stroked Lily's hair softly. She was so innocent; she had not felt the punches of the white captive. Now he felt danger in the woods. White Feather hated all Indians. If he stole a knife or rifle, he would stalk them like a hungry coyote hunting a rabbit. Just like warriors killed his mother, White Feather would kill them. As they slowly returned to the village, Mattawa kept watch, sure that the white captive was on their trail. When Bomazeen saw them emerge from the forest, he could see Lily's tear-streaked face and knew something was wrong. Mattawa ran to his father and told him the whole story.

"Where is the captive now?" he asked.

"He is still in the forest."

"I will speak to Gray Wolf. Come with me. You may need to give proof of your story."

When Bomazeen found Gray Wolf, he was in his lodge laying out roots and herbs he would need to treat fevers. Winter was coming and with it many diseases that afflicted the tribes. Red oak and wild cherry bark could be simmered for hours, rendering healing powers to cure the sick.

"Did you hear the news?" Bomazeen asked.

"I heard nothing."

"White Feather tried to kill my children. Look at Mattawa's

face. Blood flows from a wound caused by White Feather. He pushed a tree, hoping it would fall on Lily and Mattawa. My son protected his sister but injured his face. Mattawa step into the light."

Mattawa showed him the wound. By now, blood dripped down his neck onto his clothes.

"No son of mine would do that."

"He is not your son. Can't you see?"

Gray Wolf stood up from his worktable and faced the chief. "I spoke to spirit bird and he told me to capture a white boy and make him my son who will be one who hunts and fishes for my people."

"Spirit bird was wrong. Pere Rale teaches me to talk to the Great Spirit who created May-May. The captive does not belong here. Return him to his people before he kills someone. He hates you. He hates Shining Star. White Feather wants to kill all of us. He wants to kill you."

"No boy could kill me."

"White Feather could set your wigwam on fire. Both you and Shining Star would die."

"You cannot tell me what to do. Only May-May can do that. I will talk to him."

~~~~

A short time later, Bomazeen picked up a cedar log and

carried it across the village to where Father Rale worked. Side by side they cut and hammered logs to build a long house—sturdy cabin. Here was the priest's new home, a place where he could write his book. It was no ordinary book, but a book that was his life's work. Since the time he arrived in America, he had worked on a dictionary, translating native words into French. It was written neatly, with precision. As the sun set, he wrote in dim light, dipping his quill pen into an ink well and forming the letters carefully.

Father Rale wrote the definition of Wabanaki—People of the Dawn Land—in his dictionary. Here the rising sun first struck the shores, forests, and lakes of America. Every morning, the priest woke at dawn to say Mass. After Mass, he taught catechism to the children, listened to complaints and worries of the tribe. He was peacemaker and confessor. In the afternoon, he brought medicines to the sick and anointed the dying. At night, he retired to his cabin to say prayers and finally lay his head down on his fur mat and fall asleep.

~~~~

Chilly autumn days were now upon them, a time of brilliant colors, of bright leaves hanging from maple trees. Chief Bomazeen watched Lily and Running Deer pound nuts into powder, smelled salmon roast on the wood fire, and heard men chop wood to store up for the winter. Father Rale helped stack wood in neat piles under a wide shelter made of birch. In many ways, Bomazeen thought it mysterious that a white man would leave his people to live with them. How quickly he became like one of them. As they sat around campfires, Rale listened carefully and then wrote words down in his dictionary. He used those words to write a catechism in the native language.

Father Rale stood up straight and stretched; sweat covered his forehead. An idea came to him. He would build a desk on which he would work on his dictionary and write letters to his family in France. As he sipped cool water from a kettle, he noticed Bomazeen standing alone. The chief waved to meet with him — over there — in a grove of maple trees. To Bomazeen, autumn was a time of harvest, but also a time of beauty. In the morning sun all the faded leaves gleamed like golden dust. A brisk wind blew fresh and gold, causing orange and red leaves to drift lazily down onto the frost-covered hill.

"Do you know the legend of Great Bear?" Bomazeen asked.

"I have not heard it," the priest replied.

"Great Bear was a giant bear formed by stars in the night sky. Before the coming of our people to this land, a battle took place among the stars. A huntsman, also made of stars, killed Great Bear. His blood fell from the sky onto maple leaves.

That is why maple leaves are the color of blood."

"Why do you speak of this legend?" the priest asked.

"I fear war with the English. Settlers want to take our land. They lie to us in treaties and then attack our people. We can only protect our villages by fighting them to the death. Much blood will spill in these forest and fields."

Father Rale closed his eyes. He appeared to be concentrating on every word spoken by the chief. Now Bomazeen told his story.

He said, "Many moons ago, the English built a fort in Pemaquid. To the Norridgewock people, that was a declaration of war. Many in our tribe wanted war with the white settlers. I spoke for peace. Thirteen chiefs agreed with me and we paddled down the Kennebec to talk of peace. It was a great heartbreak to me that they insulted me and turned us away, but I did not give up. Before the ice-forming moon, I paddled downstream with two other braves. I got out of my canoe and walked toward the fort, holding a white flag over my head. The white men aimed rifles at my head and took us captive. We were put on a ship and sailed to Boston. For a long time, I sat in a dark prison. Often, I was sick and hungry. No rays of light came into my cell. Rats ran at my feet; fleas crawled on my body."

Chief Bomazeen raised his arms toward the cloudless blue

sky. To Father Rale, it appeared that he wanted to fly away from this earth.

"I wanted to die, but my people needed me. One day, I was released. To feel the sun on my face and breathe fresh air was like a miracle. Now you have come and that gives me hope of peace for my people. Still, I fear that you are in grave danger. The English want to kill you. Someday, you will have to return to Canada where you will be safe."

"Alas, what would become of your faith if I should abandon you? Your salvation is dearer to me than my life."

At these words, Father Rale clutched the small crucifix that hung from his neck. He held out his hand to Bomazeen. "I will stand by your side against the English. They have no right to take your fields or forests. I swear on the cross of Jesus that I will not betray you."

The two men grasped hands firmly. Both understood that taking a stand would threaten the English. They knew that much blood was to be shed, blood of the English and Wabanakis, blood of women and children.

Chapter 5
Threats

Wet leaves blanketed the forest floor and light snow fell on the fields. Wisps of fog hovered above the mountain crests and slushy snow covered the ground. A mournful smell filled the air — that of withered leaves turned dead and moldy. All year long, the Wabanakis prepared for the cold, making clothes for the bitter cold months that lay ahead. Women wore heavy robes made of animal skins and covered their feet with fur-lined boots made of moose hide. One late autumn day, Chief Bomazeen brought Father Rale a gift.

"Pere Rale, you will need snowshoes to walk on snow," the chief said, handing him snowshoes made of hides and birch. "Strap these onto your feet and try to walk. It is best to practice when little snow is on the ground."

The priest marveled at this invention. Winter in France brought cold and storms, but snowshoes were a novelty to him.

"Why did Frenchman not invent snowshoes?" he asked.

Bomazeen answered with a hint of pride in his voice. "My people are one heart with all the Great Spirit created. We must hunt in the winter. After much thought and many failures, our ancestors figured out how to walk on top of the snow."

Leather thongs were attached to the snowshoes, designed to be pulled tightly around snow boots. Rale strapped them on his boots and took a few steps, falling forward onto the wet snow. Bomazeen laughed at the sight of the Black Robe lying flat on his face. Slowly, Rale picked himself up and tried again. In a matter of minutes, he was walking smoothly.

"When the sun is high in the sky, I will call an assembly. I have a question to ask of you. Will you come?" the chief asked.

Rale tucked the snowshoes under his arm and nodded to his friend. "I will be there."

At midday, all the tribe gathered in the long house to hear the words of Bomazeen. He gazed out over his people and then turned to the priest.

"Our friend, the Black Robe, what I say to you is what all those whom you see here say to you: you know us. And you know that we are in need of provisions. We have no other resource until harvest, but to go to the shore of the sea in search of food. It would be hard for us to give up prayer; therefore, we hope that you will be disposed to accompany us, so that, while searching for food, we shall not interrupt our prayer."

Father Rale cleared his throat and consented to their request in their native language, "Kekikberba."

In one voice the people said thankfully, "Ouriounie."

Surrounded by braves, Father Rale climbed into the canoe and they glided down the Kennebec. The river glittered and sparkled with white and silver flashes. It seemed to have a voice, singing in the swiftly moving current. For the first time, Red Hawk went on the hunting trip to the shore, paddling the canoe around granite rocks and through surging white waters. It was a race against time as winter was closing in on them. All afternoon, they paddled down river in the fading sunlight. They camped next to shore. Immediately, the men planted poles in the soil and covered it with a large piece of cloth, building a portable altar. Bomazeen directed his men to place a cedar board on supports to create a make-shift altar. Father Rale laid silk cloth on the altar. It was time for evening prayer. Father Rale lit one small candle and held it over his breviary. At the conclusion of vespers, the Black Robe spread his mat under the stars. A white crescent moon hung over the mountain ridge. He pulled up a bear-skin mat and went to sleep.

Together with twenty braves, Father Rale reached the seashore and they set up camp in a stand of pine trees near the rocky shore. A fragrant smell of spruce trees and marshy earth filled the air. Red Hawk left the group to explore to the south, past a promontory and out of sight. The priest watched him depart and took a deep breath of sea air. Clams were in abundance as were bayberries for his candles. Suddenly, peace was disturbed by the call of a man thrashing through the woods. It was a member of the hunting party, breathless from running. "The English are coming. I saw them marching through the woods!"

Without delay, Bomazeen responded, "They must know that we are here with Pere Rale. Some of you will bring him back to the village. The rest will stay here and continue to hunt."

In a short time, Father Rale and his guides gathered supplies and disappeared into the woods, leaving no time to bring the chapel with them. Meanwhile, Bomazeen and his men trekked north in search of more clams, still within view of the camp.

~~~~

A short time later, Red Hawk arrived, excited to bring an armful of bayberry branches to Father Rale.

He called out, "Pere Rale, I have a gift for you."

No answer.

That is strange, Red Hawk thought. *He never strays far from the chapel.*

Upon closer examination, he saw that the priest's Mass kit and sacred vessels were gone. A terrible thought came to him:

the English have come and carried him away. His heart thudded hard against his chest. He took off into the woods to tell those in the Wabanaki village that Father Rale had been kidnapped. Swiftly, he ran through the forest groves. Red Hawk could not feel his body because of his grief. Still, he kept moving, jumping over rocks and roots, determined not to let sadness overwhelm him. A feeling rose up inside him like an inner numbness: Pere Rale could not be kidnapped; the Great Spirit would not let that happen.

Spruce trees rustled overhead. He heard the river trickling over stones. At the river he stripped bark from a tree, picked up a soft black rock, much like charcoal, and drew a picture of the English surrounding the priest and cutting off his head. He fastened the letter to a pole and drove it into the sand on the riverbank. All who passed by would learn the terrible news. With his task completed, Red Hawk ran through the forest toward Norridgewock.

The sky turned dark, covered with black storm clouds. Thunder rumbled down from the mountains. A terrible bolt of lightning flashed across the sky. Snow-white bolts hurtled down from the mountains. Now the skies opened up sending a deluge of rain, soaking Red Hawk to the bone. Blindly, Red Hawk ran through the black forest. Now he came to the river. Cold winds blew across the water, stirring it into an icy green froth. He staggered next to the riverbed. Still he kept running, running north, away from the British and home to the village. All the while, one thought filled his mind—Pere Rale was dead, beheaded by British soldiers. It felt like the world had come to an end.

The storm ended in a slow drizzle and miraculously, the sun peeked out from the clouds. The sky arched silky blue and he saw smoke rising from campfires at the village. Frantically, he raced through the village in search of Pere Rale. He was not in his cabin. He was not by the campfire. In despair, Red Hawk headed to the river. There he spotted the Black Robe, peacefully walking on the shore, reading his prayer book.

He asked, "Red Hawk, why are you in such distress?"

"Ah, Pere Rale, how glad I am to see you. My heart was dead, but it lives again on seeing you. I thought the English had captured you and cut off your head!"

He put his hand on Red Hawk's shoulder. "You must never be afraid. Trust in God. No matter what happens, trust in Him."

Chapter 6

Play Time

Bitter cold descended on the village—time to head north. Men of the village snowshoed through deep drifts to Moosehead Lake. For the first time, Mattawa joined the men on their trek north. Snow creak under his feet as he strained to keep pace with them. He could hear the brittle creaking of trees. His father had taught him that sound meant temperatures were dangerously cold. Gusts of wind blew plumes of snow off fir branches; feathery sheets of snow gleamed in the sun. Mattawa's legs ached as he trudged through deep drifts. Finally, they reached their destination and set up camp. Here the men chopped holes in thick ice, dropping bait into the frigid waters. With a yank of the line, they hauled trout up from deep waters. After filling baskets with fish, Mattawa joined his father in the hunt for moose and deer. The boy was ready for his first kill.

"Crouch here, behind this tree, and be silent. A moose will come," Bomazeen said.

They sat for a long time. Mattawa felt his toes tingle with cold. Hunting was not as exciting as he thought, but it was not the Wabanaki way to complain. Just when it felt impossible to sit any longer, he heard the crack of tree branches. In a stand of trees stood a bull moose; Mattawa held his breath. Bomazeen held up his hand to wait. The moose waded through deep drifts, out into a clearing. Still not sensing the presence of hunters, the moose walked further into the clearing. Bomazeen nodded. It was time. They burst out of the woods and raced toward their prey. Faster and faster they ran, skimming over the snow like jackrabbits, closing in on the animal. With each passing minute, the moose slowed, bogged down in deep snow until finally he had to stop.

Bomazeen motioned to kneel. Father and son put arrows to string and released. The great beast fell in billows of snow; he lay there looking up at them, still alive. Mattawa stared into the wide brown eyes and saw his own reflection. The next step was to stab him with a hunting knife; his hand froze at the thought.

"You do not want to kill this creature of the forest," the chief said. Mattawa did not answer. "The Great Spirit has sent the moose to give us food. He must die so that our people will survive. It is a gift of life and we must respect the offering of moose to us," Bomazeen said. Now the snow was covered in blood. Bomazeen put his hand on the fur and felt the beating heart.

"It is time," he said.

Mattawa plunged his knife into the animal's heart and the moose went limp. Bomazeen put a hand on his son's shoulder, "Many hard times are to come. We must be strong, even in the face of death."

Light snow fell on the men as they laid the moose on a wooden sledge and dragged it back to the village. Mattawa snowshoed behind the sledge, carrying supplies on his back. When he saw smoke rising above the pine forest, he knew they were near home.

"Can I run ahead to the village?" he asked Bomazeen.

His father nodded. "Yes. It will be a time of celebration. No longer will they suffer hunger pains."

Mattawa ran up the trail along the riverbank. Puffs of snow blew off branches as he raced through the woods, weaving between trees until he saw the village. As he entered the village, Mattawa raised his arms in triumph. People stopped their work and ran up to him. Soon the hunting party returned. Beaver pelts, fish, and the moose carcass were piled upon the sledge. That night they celebrated with a feast. Meat was stripped and hung out to dry. They roasted meat on a stick and the men beat drums; food was prepared while the children played games. Lily's favorite game was sliding flat sticks across crusty snow. Who would make their stick go farthest? Mattawa handed out smooth sticks made of pine. White Feather stood next to the campfire. Mattawa offered him a sliding stick and said the one English word he knew, "Friend?" White Feather knocked the stick to the ground and turned his back on Mattawa.

Mattawa noticed Father Rale watching them play, apparently deep in thought. Mattawa wondered what he might be thinking. He guessed that Father Rale pondered the stand-off between Gray Wolf and White Feather. Mattawa knew that Gray Wolf had said nothing to Bomazeen about returning the boy to his people. Apparently, all the priest could do was to wait and pray. Finally, Father Rale walked over to Lily.

"Lily, can I give it a try?" he asked.

"Yes, Pere Rale," she said.

"Here is a special stick for you," Mattawa said. The boy took out his hunting knife and carved a cross on one end and gave it to the priest.

"I am honored by this gift," Rale said, bowing slightly. "May I carve a cross on your stick?"

Mattawa handed him his knife and waited as the priest etched a cross, a crooked one, deep into the handle. The boy dusted away the shavings and smiled. "Now let's play."

In one sweeping motion, Father Rale skimmed the stick over

the crust until it bumped into Lily's stick and stopped. The priest laughed and slid his stick, playing with the children on this sunny winter's day. Mattawa wished this moment would never end.

Chapter 7

White Feather

Spring came to the village bringing gusts of warm air over the Kennebec River. As the frozen waters cracked, chunks of ice floated down the river. It was time for the arrival of great multitudes of fish swimming upstream to lay eggs in the ponds and shallows of the northern woods. Shad, those plump fish, answered the ancient call to fight over waterfalls and strong currents, fight to reproduce year after year. Here Sandy River and the Kennebec joined, forming a shallow, wide pool. In April, Wabanakis built weirs to trap shad in these shallows.

Gray Wolf and White Feather were first to arrive at the eddy. Gray Wolf was filled with hope that fishing the shad run would make them become like father and son. Shining Star agreed. It had been a disappointing winter. He often thought about all the trouble White Feather brought to the village. White Feather refused to learn Wabanaki words. In turn, Gray Wolf refused to learn English words. Stony silence prevailed between them. White Feather ate no meat, living on cornmeal mush. He grew thin and often remained in the wigwam, huddling by the fire. When Shining Star brought him food, he spoke angrily. "You are not my mother."

It was hard for Gray Wolf to think of White Feather as his son. He looked nothing like Swift Arrow, who had dark brown eyes and straight, black hair the color of an eagle's feather. Perhaps if White Feather did not have curly red hair and blue eyes ... his presence did not fill the hole in his heart. Gray Wolf was sure that Shining Star felt the same way.

Gray Wolf and White Feather stood in the shallows, waiting and watching. If only the boy could speak his language, Gray Wolf would tell him the thrill of seeing the first fish, glinting with green scales, splashing as it fought through the strong currents. Winter food supplies were almost gone. Roasted shad meat would fill their stomachs. Gray Wolf handed the boy a two-pronged spear to stab the fish. Downstream, a small waterfall ran over a rocky ledge. Suddenly, a fish leaped over the falls.

"They have come!" Gray Wolf shouted. Men and boys raced from the village, spears in hand, and jumped into the icy cold waters. Hundreds of fish streamed into the eddy, so full they could not move. Generations of Wabanakis harvested shad, spearing the flapping fish and tossing them ashore. For the boys, it was like a play, stabbing and splashing. White Feather stood on shore and watched, finally walking slowly back to his wigwam where he sat alone in the dark. Gray Wolf was so caught up in the hunt that he did not notice.

~~~~

Back in the village, the women prepared a large fire to roast fish. Father Rale carried wood and brush and placed it in a pile next to the fire. Just then he saw White Feather disappear into his wigwam. The priest saw Shining Star glance at him with a worried look on her face. She came over to Father Rale.

"What should we do?" she asked.

"He is thin and weak," he said. "If he does not change, he will get sick and die."

"Did all of his family die in the raid?"

"His father survived."

"Now there are two fathers with holes in their hearts." She tossed sticks into the fire and watched yellow flames send sparks into the air. Shining Star was lost in thought and came to know the hard talk she must have with Gray Wolf.

Suddenly, thick smoke filled the air. Black plumes billowed out from White Feather's wigwam. Orange and red flames burst through the wigwam, setting the bark on fire. Shining Star saw a figure running into the woods. It was White Feather, trying to escape again. A black plume of smoke rose over the village. It sent a signal to all the men fishing at the eddy. They all ran back to the village. Gray Wolf arrived just in time to see his wigwam collapse in a heap of ashes and embers. The women heaved cooking water on the last flames; the fire was out.

"What happened?" Gray Wolf asked.

"White Feather set it on fire and ran into the woods," she answered.

"I will go into the woods and capture him again. This time I will beat him. He will never do this again."

"That will make things worse. He will grow angry and more dangerous to our people."

"I have tried to teach him, but he walks away from me. Now it is time to use my fists." He clenched his hands and shook them at the smoldering ashes of his wigwam.

Shining Star desired to tell him the words of Father Rale but knew it would enrage him. The priest had told her that White Feather would not change. His father was alive; he was determined to return to his people. Jeremiah Smith would never be White Feather, never be their son. He had to go back to his people before he killed someone.

As they stared at the pile of ashes, Shining Star spoke softly. "Gray Wolf, I too grieve for our lost son and thought that the white captive would fill the hole in my heart. White Feather has made it worse. We must return him to the white settlers."

"Never!" That was his word, but it fell limply on her ear. Shining Star knew that it was only a word, a word that did not come from his heart. She knew that Gray Wolf wanted to be rid of this white boy, this pestilence that lived among them, but he did not know how to change his mind and maintain authority as medicine man.

After so many years living with Gray Wolf, Shining Star sensed all these thoughts. She had to give him a way to keep his pride. "White Feather still has a father. He escaped the raid. Although he is white, he is still human. He grieves for his son just as we long for Swift Arrow. Two fathers have holes in their hearts."

Tears brimmed in her eyes. Gray Wolf looked sadly at her and sighed. Reluctantly he said, "I will do as you wish, but only to protect my people."

Chapter 8

Ghost Cat

White Feather was a foolish, desperate boy. By all appearances, he was determined to travel hundreds of miles, back to his people, carrying only a hatchet. Little did he know that a predator had picked up his scent. Twigs cracked under the feet of a woodland creature—a creature skilled at stalking prey. At that moment, a hungry mountain lion prowled nearby in search of prey. It had been a long winter with food scarce and snow deep. Any moving creature was fair game for this lion. The Wabanakis called him Puma.

As night fell, White Feather could not have known that he was being stalked. Puma knew how to be invisible one moment, and then hurtle at his hapless victim in a split second. He was eight feet long from his black nose to the tip of his tail; light brown fur covered his sleek body. Puma could hunt in dim light; his enormous eyes allowed him to see in darkness. Stalk and ambush—that was how he hunted. Thickly padded paws enabled him to sneak through the forest undetected. Even his claws retracted at each step.

White Feather stumbled through the forest in a cacophony of snapped twigs and rustling leaves. From a short distance away, Puma perked up his ears. Slowly, he crept through thick underbrush toward his prey. His sharp ears sensed movement from another direction for Father Rale also stole through the forest in search of White Feather.

~~~~

Back at the village, it was decided that Father Rale would search for the lost boy. It was also decided that he would go alone, for Father Rale was the only one who spoke English. White Feather ran away from everyone else.

Father Rale had learned Wabanaki ways and knew how to walk quietly through the forest, alert to even the slightest sound. He heard branches snap and the sound of breathing. He also heard a human being whimpering in fear. White Feather must be nearby. Father Rale caught a glimpse of movement. He saw brown fur and a long tail. He guessed that an animal—perhaps a mountain lion—was closing in on the boy. Father Rale arrived first and stood before the lost child. White Feather did not flinch at the sight. Instead he shouted, "Go away!" This loud noise appeared to startle Puma and another creature of the forest. A white-tailed deer leaped out from behind a fir tree right into the path of the lurking mountain lion. The deer did not have a chance. In one lightning-quick instant, Puma jumped on his prey and bit cleanly into its windpipe.

Father Rale was fast too. Without saying a word, he scooped up White Feather under one arm and ran toward the village, leaving Puma behind to devour his meal. It was a mad dash through the forest. Father Rale leaped over rocks, swerved around trees with his black robe fluttering behind him. Faster he ran, all the while with his head down, careful not to trip on exposed roots. To make matters worse, White Feather kicked and scratched Father Rale, trying to break loose. Suddenly, the priest came to a giant boulder, taller than any man. I do not recognize that landmark, Father Rale thought. They were lost, and night had descended. Rain began to fall.

"We will have to wait for sunrise to find the village," Rale said.

Just then they heard the cougar cry out. It sounded like the scream of a woman being murdered. That was incentive for White Feather to cooperate.

"I will make a shelter of evergreen boughs. Can you cut some with your ax?" asked the priest.

White Feather said nothing. He simply took up his ax and hacked away at a nearby tree, creating a large pile of brush. Father Rale arranged the branches in the shape of a hut and there they settled down for the night. Father Rale was surprised to hear the boy snoring peacefully. He has been through so many tragedies, oh Lord, help us to bring him safely home to his real father. The priest knew it would be a sleepless night for him. He took up the ax and kept watch for wild animals prowling through the woods.

At daybreak, Father Rale stood next to a pine tree and listened for the sound of rushing water. If he could find the Kennebec River, it would be a simple matter of following along the riverbank. That is what they did, bedraggled boy following tired priest onward through the forest, toward the stream that lead them to Norridgewock village. All those in the village stared in wonder at their arrival. Blood trickled down the priest's face. Without saying a word, White Feather ran into a wigwam.

The people gathered in a circle around the priest. He must have a story to tell, one of a heroic rescue in the face of great danger. Running Deer brought him a bowl of wash water. Father Rale wiped blood and dirt from his face, saying nothing of the adventure. Gray Wolf was first to speak.

"Tell us what happened," he said.

"I can only say one thing. White Feather must be returned to his people. Nothing will stop him from running away again," the priest replied.

Shining Star glanced at Gray Wolf, certain that he would tell of his decision. Instead, there was silence between the two men. Gray Wolf tightened his jaw, determined to say little of the incident.

"The Great Spirit bird May-May has protected him, of that I am sure. May-May tells me that I control White Feather's fate, not you." Sparks of defiance lit his eyes. Without another word, he stomped away.

Chapter 9

Tea Time

Cotton Mather lived many miles south of Norridgewock in a place called Boston, a place considered by residents to be the center of British culture. Cotton Mather was a prosperous man, commissioner of a missionary group called the New England Company. He was also a preacher, scientist, and on this day, a man eager to rid himself of a dastardly Frenchman. That is why he called Samuel Sewall, an associate, to his office. Sewall sat in a chair across from Mather, separated only by a polished mahogany desk covered with neat piles of paper. Mather drummed his fingers on the desk and said nothing. Sewall also said nothing, waiting in deference for the commissioner to speak first. The brief interlude of silence was broken by a knock at the door. A woman entered carrying a tray beautifully arranged with a shiny silver teapot, cream, sugar and delicate china teacups decorated with tiny red rosebuds.

"Shall I pour tea for you, sir?" the woman asked. She wore a black dress, white apron and a maid's cap designed to keep servant hairs out of the tea.

"Indeed," Mather replied.

Hot, fragrant tea imbued the air, steaming as it rose from the teacup. Mather stirred cream and sugar into his tea. His first sip was always the best, a great comfort to him in these grave times of conflict. The woman poured tea for Sewall, who also added cream and sugar. His hand trembled slightly as he drank, apparently nervous about the meeting.

"Well?" Mather said.

Sewall decided to start with good news. "An Indian runner has delivered a message offering to release a boy captured in the raid on York village."

"What is his name?"

"Jeremiah Smith."

"What do they want in return?"

"I see no request for rifles or blankets."

"Strange … savages are greedy for British goods." He narrowed his eyes, pondering motives of these natives.

Sewall studied the message again. It was written in fluent English, probably by the Black Robe. "I read only that they will return the boy."

"All we can do is look for this Jeremiah Smith at our next meeting with the savages in June. I do not trust them for they break many treaties with us," he said as he leaned back in his chair. "Well? What other news?"

Sewall knew what 'well' meant. Cotton Mather probably suspected that he also had bad news. Sewall cleared his throat. "Do you wish me to start with the report of Reverend Joseph Baxter?"

"Please do," Mather said, still drumming his fingers.

Sewall began. "Joseph Baxter, loyal subject of the British crown, proper minister of the reformed Protestant religion, offered to live among the Indians, set up a school and teach the nobility of our religion."

"That was our plan. Truth is a sword that cuts to the heart, even among savages. It is a plan that cannot fail," Mather said.

Sewall squirmed in his seat. "I am sorry to say that Reverend Baxter was forced to leave."

"What do you mean?"

"The savages rejected him. Their minds have been poisoned by the Black Robe. Sebastian Rale wrote a 100-page letter in defense of the Catholic Church and sent it to Baxter."

"And did Baxter reply?"

"No, he did not have answers. Rale has a keen mind and is well-schooled in trickery. Baxter refused to answer his lies."

Mather stopped drumming. "No answer? No answers to the deceits of the Papist who prevails upon these simple, ignorant people?"

"That is what happened."

"Do you know what lies the Frenchman teaches?"

"I do not."

"I do. I interviewed one of their chiefs, Bomazeen. The Papist teaches that Jesus was French, and his mother was a French lady."

"Abominable!"

"He has entirely French-ified the savages. Moved by the instigation of the Devil, he is!"

Mather poured more tea for himself. This time he did not sip but gulped it straight down. Abruptly, he stood and went to the window, pulling frilly lace curtains to one side to peer at the street below. Horse carriages clattered along the cobblestone streets, crowded with Bostonians rushing to markets.

"It is my duty to protect the people of Massachusetts from Indian attacks," Mather said.

His mind wandered as he recalled an attack on the town of Deerfield many years ago, an attack in which the minister was killed and his family taken captive, never to return. Two hundred people died that day. The thought of it sparked a burn in his stomach. He turned and stepped over to the desk, leaning heavily over the tea tray.

"I demand deference from these natives. I demand proper symbols of good faith and a submissive spirit. They are subjects of the British crown, who allows them to live on his lands."

"What symbols of respect do you want, sir?" Sewall asked.

"At every meeting with these tribes, I want the British flag to fly on the headmost canoe. Give a full report to Governor Dudley. Tell him to write another peace treaty and summon the savages."

Sewall waited for more instructions. None came. Mather sank back into his seat and tapped his fingers together, thinking hard about the situation. "We are in a battle of good versus evil. Sebastian Rale is a conniving, deceitful man. He is evil in the flesh. Oh yes, he has created a hellish mix of Jesuit lies and Indian savagery. Don't doubt me on this. He must be eliminated. One fine day we will see his hairy scalp hanging from a post on Boston Common. This is a battle between barbarism and civility. Mark my words, our glorious British empire will triumph."

And with those words, he poured himself another cup of tea.

Chapter 10

Bomazeen Speaks

One day in the month of June, Lily went out to the cornfield with Running Deer. Green corn sprouts emerged from the moist soil. Soon the withering summer sun would beat down on the plants. It was time to hill the corn. Lily piled mounds of dirt around the stems to protect new growth. With spring rains and many sunny days, it was to be a bountiful harvest. She worked rapidly in the hot sun, eager to be finished with her work. At the last pile of dirt, Running Deer beckoned to her. "Today we will make a cornhusk doll," her mother said.

Together they sat by their hut, surrounded by a pile of dried cornhusks from last year's harvest. Her mother's hands moved swiftly, twining leather cords around bunched husks. From her work emerged the body, then arms and legs. Carefully she shaped the head and tightly sewed it to the body. Lily sat transfixed as a pile of husks became a little girl. Running Deer handed the doll to her.

Running Deer smiled and said, "She will be a friend to you, one who will comfort you at night. Your life will be like the river that flows by our village; it runs peacefully on days of little wind. On days of great storms, the river becomes dangerous, with strong currents that can sweep canoes away, even to death."

All day long, Lily thought of these words—all through their meal and as she lay on her mat at night, hugging her doll. Mosquitoes buzzed in her ears. As she swatted them, she heard the murmuring of men's voices. It sounded like a gathering around the campfire. Familiar voices spoke loud enough for her to hear.

Gray Wolf talked first. "I hear of Queen Anne, new leader of the English. She said that we are her subjects and we dwell on her land. Her land?" he gestured toward the forest. "Our people have dwelt here longer than anyone can remember. We must fight for these lands. A white man named Dudley, governor to the south, has heard our war drums and is afraid. He wants us to meet with him. No meetings! No treaties! It is time to fight for our lands and our lives."

Chief Bomazeen stood up. Light from the campfire lit up their faces, tight with fury. "My people, you are right to feel angry at the white settlers. We are not subjects of the British. This is our land. Now they tell us that all Black Robes must leave and return to Canada. They say that Father Rale stirs up hatred for the English. This is not true. He only wants us to live in peace on our own lands."

Gray Wolf's voice rose in anger. "On this point I agree with the white leader; Black Robe must leave our village. The English want to kill him and take his scalp. It is a danger to our people to have him here, for our enemy will search for him and kill us along with him."

Lily peeked out at the braves gathered around the fire. She squeezed her corn husk doll until straw fell out of its arm. Father Rale sat on a log, listening quietly. Everyone, even Lily, knew about the law banishing Jesuits from the province. Father Rale had read the edict aloud to those in the village. It was written by Governor Dudley. Father Rale's voice rose in anger at Dudley's words. The priest read, *Indians taking measures from their evil counsels and suggestions, and they are bigoted in their zeal for pernicious and damnable principles.* Father Rale explained that Dudley hated the Catholic Church. The governor tried to lure the Wabanakis away from these Catholic truths by promising them their own Protestant minister who would live among them. Loyal to the Black Robes, the Wabanakis refused.

Bomazeen spoke again. "Governor Dudley has called another meeting with our people to make our peace treaties stronger. I say that we must go. Chiefs from other tribes are going. We must stand as one people against the white man.

Tomorrow all the chiefs will meet with the white men and sign a peace treaty. A messenger from Boston has sent us a British flag that must fly on our lead canoe." He turned to Gray Wolf. "Is there anything that you wish to say?"

Gray Wolf gave the appearance of a man carved out of stone. His square jaw was rigid; his eyes fixed on the crowd. "I will not paddle a canoe with a British flag. That is final. I do have news for you," here he bellowed, not wishing to reveal the humiliation he felt from returning the boy. "I love my people. I want to protect my people. White Feather has attacked our children and burned down my wigwam. That is why I am returning White Feather to his people."

On this note, the gathering ended. Lily saw the braves push aside their war drums. Once again, her father had spoken, and his people had listened. White Feather was going back to his people. This made her happy. Now she could play in the forest without fear of another attack. Lily sneaked back to her mat and kissed her doll. Soon she was fast asleep.

Chapter 11

Confrontation

The next day Lily smoothed the straw of her doll's face and whispered to her, "Today is the Feast of Corpus Christi. It is the day we celebrate the hidden Jesus in the holy bread. My mother has made me new clothes of blue cloth. Look at the beads she has sewn to my dress and onto my leggings. She said it is our way of honoring the Great Spirit and His son."

After dressing, she went out to the church where her people gathered. Mattawa was already wearing his black and white cassock, brought all the way from France. Ten altar boys formed a line, each holding a flickering candle. Father Rale wore white vestments and took his place at the head of the procession. As Holy Mass neared the consecration, Lily watched the priest's every move and listened to the foreign sound of Latin spoken at the consecration. He raised the Host and Mattawa rang little gold bells.

Sometimes Lily thought the Host looked like a full moon, hidden by clouds; God was always with her in the Host. She did not see him, but He was there. She hugged her doll and thought of her mother's words. Even Bomazeen did not know what tomorrow would bring. All the people knelt and prayed for peace. Soon afterwards, Bomazeen stood by the river, ready to head south to the shores of New Casco Bay. Dressed in a colorful headdress filled with feathers, his face was painted in bright reds and yellows. Four braves held the canoe steady for the priest as he approached. The riverbank was still muddy from spring rains. As his shoes squished in the mud, he slipped and fell.

Bomazeen helped him to his feet. "Are you hurt, Pere Rale?"

"Just my pride," Father Rale, said, scraping off the mud. "I will look dirty in front of the governor, but there is nothing I can do about it." He shrugged and stepped into the boat. White Feather stood at the water's edge.

"We no longer will call you White Feather. It is time for you to return to your people. Now Jeremiah, sit in the canoe with me,"

Mattawa and Red Hawk watched the departure.

"Do you think he will smile or wave good-bye?" Mattawa asked.

"He never smiles," Red Hawk said.

"I will wave to him," Mattawa said and called out. Jeremiah faced them, parting his lips, but it was not a smile. Instead, yellow teeth protruded from his mouth, just like a rat. One of the braves pushed them from shore, catching a swift current and gliding them downstream, out of sight.

The Kennebec River was peaceful that day, its banks were lined with oak and pine trees that stretched high into blue sky. Weeping willows hung over the waters. Despite clear weather, the woods were silent and somber, casting sadness over the priest's heart. He made the Sign of the Cross and kissed the crucifix of his rosary beads, shiny and black, given to him at his ordination. It was a gift from his parents who had died several years ago. Every Hail Mary reminded him of his parents, such holy people who taught him all his prayers.

As they paddled closer to their destination, more tribes appeared, chiefs of many villages all dressed in bright colors, appeared in Casco Bay. Bomazeen sat in the lead canoe, flying the British flag.

~~~~

Atop the hill overlooking these waters stood Governor Dudley dressed in a blue suit with a silk shirt, standing with a regiment of redcoats. All was as he wished. Even the weather was calm — a perfect day for signing the peace treaty. A British flag was fastened to the lead canoe; it fluttered in the breeze. He surveyed the canoes in search of Jeremiah Smith. After a short time, Dudley spotted the boy sitting in the last canoe with his head down. Dudley was pleased and ordered a welcoming salute of guns that was returned by rifle fire from their visitors. Swiftly, they landed on shore and climbed out, leaving Rale in full view of the British. A frown passed over the governor's face. He turned toward his commanding officer, Colonel Henry Penhallow.

Penhallow did not notice the expression on Governor Dudley's face. He was busy brushing lint off his regimental uniform, a uniform he wore proudly. His white shirt gleamed in the morning sun; the flashy red jacket had yellow and white stripes, accented by smoky gray trousers. He towered over all those around him. He cut a striking figure in full uniform. It helped that he had the noble bearing of an officer, complete with a high, narrow forehead and large nose that closely resembled a triangle.

Dudley glowered at Penhallow. "Do you see who is with them?"

Penhallow narrowed his eyes in disgust. "Everything was going perfectly until he showed up," he muttered.

"Pay small attention to the Black Robe," Dudley advised. "Let us carry on. Take the boy over to the guards. They will protect him in case the Indians change their minds and try to recapture him."

Without further ado, Governor Dudley spoke to the tribes through an interpreter, "Queen Anne sends messages of peace to all the tribes. If we should happen to have war with the French, remain neutral, leave us to settle our quarrels with each other. We will supply all your wants, we will take your fur, and we will trade you our goods at a reasonable price."

Dudley was sly. He knew the Wabanakis valued cloths, metal pots, and tools. It was time for the chiefs to deliberate among themselves. Chief Bomazeen gathered the tribes together, away from the British.

Father Rale was left standing alone. Dudley motioned to Penhallow. "Go and tell him I want to speak to him alone."

"Yes, sir," Penhallow replied and walked briskly over to the priest. Immediately, he spotted the muddy black robe. Penhallow was careful not to brush against the robe, lest he taint his immaculate uniform.

"Governor Dudley wishes to speak to you in private," Penhallow said.

"What does he wish to know?" Rale answered.

"That is between you and the governor. Follow me."

Reluctantly, Father Rale complied.

Governor Dudley got right to the point. "Do not influence the Indians to make war on the English," he said.

"I do not come to make war. I am a priest and seek only peace, but you must respect Indian lands," he replied.

Suddenly, Chief Bomazeen appeared. "Why do you speak to

Pere Rale? He has no weapon to defend himself. Once you took me prisoner when I sought peace. I know that you want his scalp."

"We do not want to kill anyone. I told you, we want peace," Dudley said.

"That is a lie. I do not trust you, but the Wabanakis have no choice. French soldiers will not protect us. France has withdrawn all military aid. We must sign the treaty," he said.

Bomazeen gestured to his people to gather in a circle, instructing them to pick up stones and build a pillar that was a symbol of peace called Two Brothers. Dudley placed a large stone next to the pillar, and each officer then placed stones, building a second pillar.

It was time for Bomazeen to speak.

"If you declare war on the Frenchman; know that he is my brother. We have the same prayer and we are in the same wigwam. If you enter the wigwam, I watch you from the mat where I am seated. If I see that you carry a hatchet, I will be suspicious and stand up. If you raise your hatchet to strike my brother, the Frenchman, I take my own, and run toward the Englishman to strike him. Could I see my brother struck in my wigwam, and I remain silent on my mat? No, no, I love my brother too well not to defend him. Therefore, I say to you, great captain, do nothing to my brother, and I shall do nothing to you; remain quiet on your mat, and I shall remain at rest on mine."

Dudley had no answer to these words. In fact, it surprised him that Bomazeen could speak so eloquently. After all, he still thought of them as savages, for no civilized man would paint his face and wear feathers. In his mind, Sebastian Rale was a fool to live with the Wabanakis, eating their food and living in the woods. Still, it was time to sign a peace treaty. It was all just one big act, so let the façade continue.

He gestured to his soldiers. "Fire off a volley to celebrate peace between the British Empire and the Indians."

Soldiers aimed at the clouds and shot a round of bullets in the air. Birds flew off in alarm; the air filled with smoke. As the Wabanakis began to paddle away in their canoes, Dudley's face turned red with anger. In defiance of the treaty, he nudged the pillar of Two Brothers. Rocks tumbled to the ground, creating a lumpy pile of stone. Gray Wolf saw him kick the rocks; white hot anger flashed inside him. The medicine man waded into the water near the lead canoe, ripped the British flag off the bow and tossed it ashore.

Chapter 12

The Cross

That spring and summer, peace did reign in the Norridgewock village. It was a time of planting squash, beans and corn in the fertile soil near the banks of the Kennebec River. Often, Father Rale left his cabin to pray by the river. Through days of tranquility and war, summer and winter, the Kennebec became a part of him. On stormy days, it flashed white in swirls of chaos; through the dark green forest, it raced in torrents, sparkling in silver light. It roared and thundered, like the voice of God in the days of Moses. The priest listened. He felt the British closing in, building forts ever closer to Wabanaki lands. The Kennebec River was the dividing line between New France and New England and in that sense, it was a battleground. The time had come to build stockades around the village to protect them from invasions.

Father Rale chopped trees and split logs shoulder to shoulder with the men of the village. Freshly cut pine logs had a sweet smell that emanated from the sap within. By day's end, his black robe was covered in sawdust; his hands were tough and calloused. One afternoon, he stopped for a break from the hot sun, sipping cool water from an iron kettle. Bomazeen joined him.

"I cut and drag logs from the woods. My mind is filled with one thought," Bomazeen said, and then there was a long pause. "The stockade will not protect us from attacks. One soldier can throw a flaming pine bough and burn it down. We all know the white men want your scalp. Pere Rale, for your safety, you must move back to Canada."

The priest wiped sweat from his brow. He answered without hesitation. "I will never leave my flock."

"The white men hate you. They say that you are evil and spread lies about them," he said.

Father Rale spoke calmly. "After living so many years among you, living in the wilderness, I no longer feel like a Frenchman. I assure you that I see, that I hear, that I speak only as one of you. I will not abandon my people."

Now they turned back to work building the stockade. Father Rale raised an ax and split log after log. Bomazeen cut in perfect harmony with his friend. In the days that followed, men of the village erected the high stockade that enclosed all the wigwams and cabins. A short distance away stood the church and a small schoolhouse. On the last day, Father Rale called all the people to gather in front of the church.

He raised his voice and said, "Several weeks ago, a runner

came down from Quebec with a gift. He brought this metal cross, taller than even you," he pointed at Bomazeen. "Let us now plant it in the soil and pray that the cross of Jesus is planted in our hearts ... Mattawa and Red Hawk, the time has come."

They appeared from behind the church carrying the cross. Together they dug a deep hole in the rocky soil, down through the dry topsoil, down further to dark, loose soil and drove the cross into place, securing it with rocks around its base. At last, they shoveled dirt on top and packed it down. More plans filled his mind. To the south they would build an outdoor altar to the Blessed Virgin and to the north an altar dedicated to the Guardian Angels.

That night, Father Rale lit a candle that sat on his writing table. It was a sturdy table made of pine. Many days he worked on this table, often thinking of his family back home in France. As he paused to compose his thoughts, golden light danced on the paper; it mesmerized him. He pictured the face of his brother, Pierre. Suddenly, he felt a deep longing to walk in the pastures of northern France, his boyhood home. He and Pierre often ran together through the tall grass, to an overlook where they could see the Swiss Alps. It seemed like a whole other life. He dipped his pen into the inkwell and began to write.

Should I be pitied because I am often exposed to the cold, because I endure hunger, thirst, or because I am threatened at any moment to be devoured by wild beasts? Well, these threats will force me always to keep my soul in order to be ready to present it to my Lord at a moment's notice. I fear neither iron nor fire, nor even a cruel death. I will be well rewarded, even if subjected to much suffering, should I have the joy of baptizing even one dying child.

He continued to write. *Doubtless you will judge that I have most to fear from the English gentlemen. It is true that they long ago resolved upon my death; but neither their ill will toward me, nor the death with which they threaten me, can ever separate me from my flock.*

Father Rale blew out the candle and crawled over to his bearskin mat. Fatigue overcame him. He drifted off to sleep, listening to the lonesome howls of coyote prowling the northern woods.

Chapter 13

War Drums

Lily knelt in the field picking blueberries. It was July — time to pick berries and catch eels from the river. She loved this field set on a hill, a field carpeted with blueberries, a field that ran down to the Kennebec River. Wildflowers waved in a gentle breeze, visited by butterflies flitting from blossom to blossom. Down by the shore, a canoe appeared, navigated by men not of their village. Lily watched the scene unfold. With haste, the men beached their canoe and ran up the hill carrying urgent messages from Quebec, messages for Bomazeen, who was headed for the river carrying a spear to catch eels. Little time was spent in greeting for soon they were embroiled in a serious conversation. Often, Bomazeen shook his head and seemed to disagree with the men. It appeared that he had no desire to believe them but lost that battle. The chief raised his spear, jammed it into the ground, and walked away.

Deep in thought, Lily continued to pick blueberries, but an uneasy feeling settled in her stomach. Something was wrong, but she did not know what it might be. It did not take long for her to find out. By nightfall, two hundred braves gathered, carrying tomahawks, rifles, bows and arrows. In the center of the village a huge kettle was set on the cooking fire and chunks of raw meat were tossed in boiling water. Warriors danced and beat drums, exhorting each man to be brave in battle. Lily could not eat. She saw Mattawa standing away from the fire, watching the war dance. Lily knew that he could explain to her why the Wabanakis were going to war. Sparks from the fire shot into the air and the heat was intense. Lily moved away from the circle of warriors and stood next to her brother.

"What is happening?" she asked.

"Runners came from Quebec with news that France is at war with England. The French are our friends. We will fight against the English. In this way, too, we will protect Pere Rale," he explained.

Lily surveyed the village. "Where is Pere Rale?"

"He is standing alone in the dark, holding a candle."

Lily could see his face in the light of a flickering candle; his lips were moving in prayer. It appeared to her like the whole world had dropped away from him and he was not on this earth but talking to God. She knew that he must be praying for peace. That was a word he always spoke. "Peace I leave with you. My peace I give you." Pere Rale taught them the words of Jesus. He blew out the candle and walked toward the circle of warriors. In the light of a bonfire, he raised his arms for silence.

"My brothers, I speak to you with a sorrowful heart, a heart that desires peace. I hear these war drums and know that you all are going to battle. Some of you will die. Die as holy men. Devote yourselves to prayer and practice no cruelty; kill no one except in the heat of battle. If you take prisoners, treat them kindly. Tomorrow we will set aside a day for confessions."

~~~~

The next day brought much activity to the village. Canoes were dragged to shore and filled with weapons and food. Bomazeen was first in line for confession, followed by a long line of warriors. Gray Wolf stood alone, sharpening his tomahawk. Red war paint streaked his face, coloring his cheeks with the fierce look of an eagle swooping on its prey. Shining Star approached him, knowing that she may never see him again.

"I must tell you good news." She patted her stomach, hidden beneath deerskin robes. "At the time of the ice-forming moon, we will hear the wail of a baby in our wigwam."

"You mean?"

"Soon you will see the face of an infant who will bring joy

back into our lives."

Gray Wolf stopped sharpening his tomahawk. "I wish you had not told me this now."

"I thought you would want to know in case something happens."

"I am going to kill white men. That is my one thought," he threw his tomahawk into the canoe and said nothing more. A short time later, the men guided their canoes past rocks, caught swirling waters, and headed south.

That day was a day worse than anyone could have imagined. Every able-bodied warrior from every eastern tribe descended on the English settlers, killing anyone who stood in their path, burning villages and forts. All this devastation took one day. Soon the warriors returned with salvaged goods from the settlements. In addition to their booty, they took another white captive; she sat motionless in the bottom of the canoe. Lily saw them coming around the river bend and ran down to shore. Bomazeen paddled his canoe to shore and stepped onto land. His arms were splattered with blood and he did not look at Lily. A young girl sat in his canoe. She looked to be five years old. Her yellow hair was dirty and uncombed; she wore torn clothes and her eyes were cast down. When she refused to move, a brave struck her in the head.

Bomazeen raised his voice in anger, "Do not hit her. She is just a child." He held out his hand to the girl, who timidly accepted and stepped ashore. Her face was black with soot, marked with streaks where tears had flowed down her face.

"Where is her mother?" Lily asked.

"She has no family. They are all dead," Bomazeen said. Another white captive had come to their village. The little girl trembled at the sight of so many strange faces.

Chapter 14

Dorothy

That night, the braves built a fire, raised a pole nearby and pierced it with a victorious tomahawk. In one great circle the men smoked pipes and ate boiled meat, talking loudly of the battle and the many rifles now in their possession. Running Deer sat next to the little captive and offered her food. She refused. Running Deer attempted to pat her on the head. The white girl pulled away, curling up on the ground in a ball, her face hidden by long strands of dirty yellow hair.

Running Deer turned to Lily. "Go and get Pere Rale."

Lily ran into the church where she found the Black Robe deep in prayer with his head down. He did not seem to hear her tiptoe up to him nor did he sense that she stood behind him. For many minutes, she stood and waited, but still he prayed. Lily whispered and still was not heard; she walked in front of him in hope that he would see her. Lily stood in awe at the sight of his face, so wet with tears, so unlike men of the village who were trained not to cry. Life in the wilderness required strict control over every emotion. Father Rale raised his head and was startled to see her standing next to him.

"What is it, my child?" he asked.

"We need help with the white captive. She will not eat or let us get near her."

Without answering, he genuflected before the tabernacle and hurried out of church. When he arrived at the bonfire, the girl was still curled up on the ground, not responding to any human voices. The priest crouched down next to her and gently spoke in English. "Dear child, we will not hurt you. Running Deer will care for you like you were her own daughter. Do not be afraid. Jesus is with you. Come with me."

At the sound of her native language, the child lifted her head. Father Rale reached out his hand and she gripped it tightly, struggling to her feet, but she fell. Three times she stood and fell, weakened by shock and hunger. Her legs were scratched by thorns from attempts to escape the raid on the village. Although her eyes were open, they were unseeing, turned inward. With utmost care, he picked her up and carried her to the longhouse where Running Deer had prepared warm bath water; Lily held a pile of clean clothes.

"This is Running Deer and Lily. They will bathe you and give you clean clothes. You can trust them," he said then left.

Lily watched as her mother poured water over the child's body, wiping away dirt and dried blood. Never before had Lily seen such white skin and long golden hair. Briars were tangled in the strands, making it difficult to comb. When the bath was completed, Running Deer dressed her in soft deerskin clothing with a long skirt and tunic that slipped over her head. It was embroidered with beads and had matching moccasins and leggings. Father Rale knocked and entered carrying a bowl of warm cornmeal pudding, sweetened with maple syrup. Steam rose from the pottery bowl, giving it a pleasant appearance. He scooped a small amount of pudding with a wooden spoon and held it to her lips. She turned her head away. He spoke to her in English.

"My name is Pere Rale, and this is Running Deer and her daughter Lily. Please let us help you." She kept her eyes downcast. Father Rale gestured to Lily, who took the spoon and hummed a lullaby. For the first time, the child showed interest. Lily held out the spoon and nodded to try it. Cautiously, the white girl took a tiny bite, then another and another until the bowl was empty. Next to Lily's mat, Running Deer prepared a soft mat for the captive. They laid down their heads and Lily hummed her lullaby, only to see tears trickling down the girl's face. Lily peeked down at her doll and knew what she had to do. She tucked the doll in the girl's arm and continued to hum until the captive fell asleep.

Lily woke up the next morning to find the white girl staring into space, every limb shaking with fever, her face sickly pale with dark circles under her eyes. Suddenly, the girl moaned loudly, and Running Deer came to the mat, wiping her hot forehead with a damp cloth and moistening her lips with cool water. Father Rale appeared at the door.

"How is she doing?" he asked.

"Not well. A fever has taken hold. I don't see deep wounds, only scratches. Still it looks to me that she has no hope, that she wants to give up her spirit and die," Running Deer replied.

"I believe this to be shock from the horror that she witnessed yesterday," he said, and then he spoke softly to the child in English. "What is your name?" She stirred at the familiar sound,

"Dorothy," she murmured. So deathly ill was the girl, it was like a corpse speaking.

"Dorothy, you can trust me and all the people here. You must trust Jesus. I am a priest of the Roman Catholic Church. Through the Holy Spirit, I would like to baptize you."

Dorothy's breathing slowed, and she lay motionless. Father Rale put on a purple stole and opened a small black box, taking out two glass bottles—one of holy water and the other of blessed oil. With three slow motions he said these words:

"*Ego te baptizo in nomine Patris, et Filii, et Spiritus Sancti. Amen.*"

He put holy oil on his thumb and made tiny crosses on her forehead, lips, and chest. It smelled of the balsam woods.

"Dorothy cannot be alone. It is important to give her water and try a little food," he said, turning to Lily. "Can you do this?"

"I will."

"Good. Now I will teach you some English words. It is familiar to her and makes her feel safe. It is one sentence. "My name is Lily. I am your friend."

At first, Lily stumbled over the strange language, but within several minutes she was able to say the words. Now she sat. That was it—she sat by Dorothy's side, humming little songs and saying prayers. Sometimes she closed her eyes and pictured Mary, mother of Jesus, sitting by their side. It was like a painting in her head, a magical painting in which Mary came alive. She was dressed in a pure white robe and had dark skin like her people. often raising her eyes to heaven.

"I love you," Lily said to Mary and the lady in white smiled.

Running Deer came with water and more sweetened cornmeal mush. For hours they soothed her forehead with cool cloths and tried to get her to sip water, but the child tightened her lips, turning away. Lily's mother left and returned with a bowl of beads that children used for games. One side of each bead was black, and the other side was white. Lily loved this game; she shook them out in a bowl and spilled them on the ground, trying to get all one color in each toss. That afternoon, the hut was filled with the sound of beads clattering while Lily hummed, absorbed in her game. She did not notice any movement on the mat. Her game was interrupted by coughing. Dorothy watched her play.

Lily put down the beads. "My name is Lily and I am your friend."

Dorothy tried to speak, but no sound came out. Lily poured a few drops of water onto a spoon and wiggled the spoon passed the cracked lips, relieved to see that the water went down her throat. "Water," Dorothy said in English and Lily understood. "Water," Lily said in English and gave her another spoonful, then more food until the bowl was empty. To Lily, this was like a miracle. When Dorothy finished drinking, her eyes moved in curiosity. The lodge must have appeared strange to her. Down one hall were rows of bunk beds. Bundles of herbs hung from the ceiling; across one beam hung dried pumpkins and squash. Yellow corn drooped down from roof poles, remnants of last year's harvest.

Lily tried to imagine what it was like to be Dorothy. It was impossible for her to think of seeing her parents killed. It was impossible for her to think of being taken from all that was familiar to live with strangers far away from home. Dorothy stopped watching and closed her eyes. Outside the lodge, Lily heard the women talk of going to the fields to pick corn. It felt strange to be closed up in the lodge, alone with her thoughts. To her great relief, the door opened, and Father Rale appeared, letting in fresh air and sunshine. He knelt next to the sick child and put his hand on her forehead. Lily backed away, holding her doll.

"No fever," he said. "It is time for her to get up and walk."

He leaned over and spoke in English, "Dorothy, stand up. I will help you."

Father Rale picked her up and placed her feet on the ground, only to have her thin, pale legs crumble under the weight of her own body. Three times, he propped her up; three times she fell. On the fourth try, she stood on her own, but wobbled and fell back into his arms. One step at a time, they slowly walked out of the lodge, through the door, and into bright sunshine. Dorothy squinted and covered her eyes. Long golden hair flopped over her face and became a place to hide. All the dark faces, strange language, new smells of boiling meat seemed to make her hands shake.

She cried, "Mama … Papa … Mama … Papa!"

Lily did not understand the words, but she still knew what was happening. "Mama…Papa…" Over and over the child cried until Lily thought her own heart would break. She squeezed Cornsilk. Now an idea struck her. She strode over to the little girl and handed her the doll. Dorothy threw Cornsilk to the ground. Maybe this is not a good idea, Lily thought, but she tried again. This time, Lily called her by name.

"Dorothy ... Dorothy."

The child heard her name and stopped yelling. Tears still dribbled down her face; her eyes were swollen from crying. She started to hiccup and heave deep breaths that made her body shudder. Lily made the little doll sing and dance to catch her attention. Like the sun bursting out from behind a dark cloud, Dorothy smiled just a tiny bit. Lily gestured for her to hold the doll and she did. Now Lily pointed for her to sit on a stump of wood. Running Deer brought her water, which she drank in huge gulps.

Father Rale observed all of this and finally spoke to Lily. "Water and food will give her strength. Bring her up to the cornfield. I think that she would like to see the wildflowers and watch butterflies. Here are four new words: 'Come play with me'." Lily quickly caught on to the English words.

"Come play with me," Lily said and held out her hand.

Dorothy slipped her hand into Lily's hand and together they walked up to the field. Platforms had been built as lookouts to scare away crows. Lily helped her climb up and they gazed out over the fields. Corn tassels waved in the wind as far as the eye could see. Sunshine fell on the child's pale face and a gentle breeze blew her hair. Down below, women pulled up weeds and picked ripe green ears of corn. Lily wondered if it might be familiar to her. Perhaps the white settlers planted corn too. Perhaps her father and mother planted ... Lily stopped thinking. It was too painful for her to think of the child's loss. Suddenly, Dorothy started to cry again.

"Come play with me," Lily said and began to climb down the ladder. They walked through the field; cornstalks towered over them, rustling in the breeze. Lily played hide-and-go-seek. That game made Dorothy laugh. When they paused, Lily listened to crows flying overhead, cawing and swooping down to steal corn. Lily flapped her arms and scared them. Dorothy flapped her arms weakly, like a young bird trying to fly away. To Lily, it appeared like the child really thought she could fly away, leaving the world behind. All these events created a crack inside of her, a crack in which she felt the pain of a child who had seen her parents murdered. Lily hid behind a thick stand of cornstalks and tears began to fall. Dorothy pulled aside the stalks in time to see Lily crying. She held up Cornsilk and gently handed it to her new friend. Lily wiped tears away and extended her hand.

"Come with me." They walked together down to the village. Dorothy ate more porridge and went into the lodge to take a nap, hugging Cornsilk tightly. She drifted off into a peaceful sleep.

Chapter 15

Near Death

Shining Star felt the raw chill of winter fast approaching. The ground was covered with slushy snow and withered leaves; an ice-forming moon rose high in the night sky. Silently, she lay on her bearskin mat listening to the breathing of Gray Wolf. In the next instant she felt the first pain low in her womb. This brought joy for soon she would hold a newborn with skin pink and pure like the petals of a wild rose. Shining Star nudged her husband. "It is time."

Awakened from a deep sleep, Gray Wolf wrapped a moose hide robe around himself, stumbling in the dark to Bomazeen's cabin. Running Deer knew more about childbirth than any woman in the village. Gray Wolf knocked on the door. "It is time," he said. Accustomed to these calls for help, Running Deer quickly dressed and hurried to their wigwam. Her first glance at the woman in labor caused tension in her stomach. Labor was proceeding rapidly, bringing waves of severe pain. Despite the cold, Shining Star was drenched in sweat. Gray Wolf stood outside the wigwam waiting to hear the first whimper of his child. A short time passed, bringing the passage of the infant out of the womb and into the night air. After one more push, the baby slid into Running Deer's hands, but something was wrong; the baby did not cry. Running Deer wrapped the child in a blanket and studied the tiny face. It was not pink, but blue.

She called out to Gray Wolf. "Run and get Pere Rale."

Gray Wolf heard desperation in her voice and ran to the priest's cabin, pounding on the door. Father Rale gathered his box that held holy oil and holy water. He tucked it under his arm and ran to the wigwam. A crack of moonlight shone through an opening in the wigwam, revealing a silent newborn and a weeping woman. He put his hand on the baby's chest and felt movement. Without a word he put on his purple stole and began the baptismal rite.

"What name do you give your child?"

"It is a girl. I wish to give her the name Marie, petite Marie, after the mother of Jesus."

Three times he poured drops of holy water on the baby's head, "*Ego te baptizo in nomine Patris et Filii et Spiritus Sancti. Amen.*"

Now he anointed Marie with holy oil, giving her the Last Rites of the Catholic Church. "Let us pray that Marie will live to run and play, to breathe the fresh air of God's good earth."

He knelt on the dirt floor and prayed, "*Pater Noster…*"

Outside the tent, Gray Wolf muttered, "Black Robe can do nothing to save my child. He says foolish prayers that do no good."

Silence fell on the scene. Gray Wolf saw the first band of golden light rise on the eastern hill. As the sun rose, the infant cried. Marie cried weakly at first, but soon she sounded robust and strong. Father Rale opened the flap on the wigwam and beckoned to the medicine man. Gray Wolf saw Shining Star holding the infant in a warm blanket. She pulled the cloth away from the baby's face, causing Marie to squirm. Gray Wolf put his big brown hand on the soft skin of his daughter. He touched the tiny head covered with shiny black hair.

Word spread quickly in the village of the events surrounding the birth of petite Marie. Mattawa and Red Hawk listened to the talk and wondered about what really happened.

"Old women gather sticks for the fire, talking of her birth. Some say that Marie died and was brought back to life by Pere Rale," Mattawa said.

"I do not know how long Marie could be blue and still live," Red Hawk said.

"Gray Wolf had to run across the village to Pere Rale's cabin."

"Time enough for a child to die."

"I do not know what to think."

"Pere Rale says to praise God that the child lived. He says nothing more. Shining Star rocks her baby and gazes at the child all day."

"Where is Gray Wolf? I have not seen him since the birth."

"He gathers bark in the woods for medicine and talks to no one."

"Gray Wolf has a hard heart. I don't think he will ever change," Mattawa said.

Chapter 16
Broken

A short time later, Father Rale stepped out of his cabin and breathed deeply of cold air that settled over the village. He had finished morning prayers and was ready to work. Thanks be to God, he thought, the chapel is built. One last detail and it is finished. Runners from Quebec had brought him a metal cross to nail over the entrance. Mattawa volunteered to help. "Pere Rale, you have waited for this moment for a long time. I will hold the ladder, but be careful, it might be slippery."

The priest climbed slowly up the ladder, using one hand to hold the cross and the other hand to grip the ladder, crudely made of oak. He had a hammer and nails in the deep pocket of his robe. He glanced down at Mattawa, who had a worried expression. Finally, Rale reached the top and dug into his pocket for the tools. That is when it happened. As he leaned back slightly, his foot slipped, and he began to fall backwards. Desperately, he grasped for the ladder. For an instant, he teetered in mid-air and tried to push toward the church hoping that he would fall securely against the building, but it was too late. He continued to fall backward and crashed to the ground, still holding the cross. There he lay motionless, like a dead man. Mattawa hollered for help and ran over to him. Please God, spare the life of our holy priest, he prayed. A crowd soon formed around the still body. Bomazeen pushed his way through and knelt next to his friend. He put his ear on Rale's chest.

Bomazeen stood up and announced. "His heart beats and he is breathing. Now we must pray."

Every man, woman, and child bowed their heads and made the Sign of the Cross. Everyone prayed except one man.

~~~~

That man was Gray Wolf. He did not pray to this strange God. No, he was pleased that the priest fell. In fact, Gray Wolf hoped that the priest would die. If he died, the English would not come to their village and try to kill this Frenchman and burn their village. Shining Star believed that Black Robe had saved his child. That was impossible for he used no healing herbs and said chants that made no sense. In fact, Gray Wolf believed that he was the only one who knew how to protect Marie by asking May-May to rid the village of this priest.

Suddenly, he heard Bomazeen call his name. *He wants me to help this cursed man*, he thought, *I would rather see him die.* As these thoughts roiled inside him, the people opened a path for him. Now it was too late to escape this task. If he left, it would appear that he was afraid. As medicine man, this would be intolerable. As he made his way toward the stricken man, all eyes were upon him. He knelt next to Rale and took out his hunting knife, ripping the robe wide open. Upon close examination, it was obvious that Rale had a fractured leg. It was swollen and broken at an angle that would make it difficult to snap back in place. Gray Wolf was not sure what to do. Everyone around him was praying, which made it difficult to think. Father Rale moaned. He was waking up and now was in pain. In order to move the bones back into place, the priest would have to be asleep. Even for a strong man like Rale, the pain would be unbearable.

Gray Wolf stood up and spoke to the crowd. "This man has a broken left leg. I will have to crack his bones, but first I need to brew up sleeping medicines. Nobody touch him until I return."

Back at his tent, Gray Wolf studied his shelf of roots and herbs, neatly arranged on wooden boards. He started a fire and heated water until it bubbled. As steam rose from the pot, he sprinkled ground herbs into the water and stirred. Many minutes passed as the brew darkened to a deep black. All was ready, except his mind. Now it was a matter of his honor in the village. If he saved the priest, all would esteem him. He opened the flap of his tent and walked slowly, carrying the brew and a small spoon. Father Rale resembled a dead man; all color had drained from his face and he remained perfectly still.

Gray Wolf bent over him. "Lift his head."

Bomazeen gently cradled Rale's head. Over the course of many minutes, Gray Wolf patiently administered small drops of medicine. As he did, Rale's body relaxed, and he fell asleep. Bomazeen and his strongest braves carried him back to Gray Wolf's tent. Would the medicine wear off? The medicine man did not know. If it did, the pain would be unbearable. The bone stuck out through the skin. Gray Wolf had moved plenty of bones in his day, so he knew bone structure well. Just as he felt around the leg, Rale opened his eyes.

"You broke your leg and I must move it. I must give you more medicine to dull the pain."

Rale mumbled weakly, "No."

"No man can stand the pain."

"No."

People will hear him scream and think I am killing him, Gray Wolf thought.

"No."

It was useless to try to convince him.

Gray Wolf stuck a piece of cloth in his mouth. "Bite down hard."

In the flickering light of a wood fire, Gray Wolf gripped the leg and slid the bone inside the skin. Rale closed his eyes and bit down. His next move was to maneuver the bone into place — painful beyond words.

"Do you want medicine?"

He shook his head no.

Expertly, Gray Wolf gripped the leg and in one strong motion snapped the bone back in place. Once again, Rale closed his eyes and bit down.

"Now I will give you medicine."

Gray Wolf removed the cloth. As he did, the priest began to mumble. The medicine man leaned down to listen.

Father Rale said, "I offer my suffering to God that He will have mercy on you. I pray that you will accept Our Lord Jesus as your Savior."

Gray Wolf lifted the priest's head and spooned a sleeping potion into his mouth. As he did, his hands trembled. Never before had he heard such prayer — a prayer directed at him.

Chapter 17

Ultimatum

Several years passed after that terrible fall from the ladder, during which time it was obvious that Father Rale would never fully recover. He walked with a limp and was forced to lean on an oak walking stick to take weight off his leg. His brown hair and beard were flecked with gray. It was impossible for him to carry heavy objects. Often, he grimaced in pain—as if he bore hidden pains. Years of reading and writing by dim light had blurred his vision. It had become his habit to rub his tired, red-rimmed eyes. Over time, many changes came to the village. At the age of ten, Dorothy, still thin and weak, asked to live with a French family in Quebec. She never adjusted to their food and their hard way of life. Father Rale also suspected that she could not overcome the shock of seeing her parents killed in the raid. At the sight of a brave in war paint, she retreated to the lodge and curled up on her mat, refusing to talk. On the day of her departure, Lily stood on the riverbank and watched her canoe round the bend. Dorothy did not glance back. Lily did not cry because she was now a strong young woman who had fallen in love with Red Hawk, who had grown into a handsome brave. Red Hawk put his arm around Lily and hugged her tenderly.

One thing did not change. Tensions increased between the English and all tribes of the eastern forests. It was true that the French and British governments had signed a peace treaty, ending the Queen Anne's War. In that treaty, England claimed ownership of all lands inhabited by the tribes and declared them subjects of the British Empire. More forts were built, closer and closer to lands owned by the tribes.

As was a daily habit, Father Rale spent time writing letters. He wrote to his family in France and to his Jesuit superior in Quebec, informing him of his mission. He was interrupted by a knock at the door. It was Bomazeen.

"Pere Rale, I must talk to you."

Father Rale put down his pen. "You look angry, my friend. How can I help?"

"I do not trust the great chief of the English. The peace treaty says they want to live peaceably with my people. Is it to live in peace with me to take my land against my wishes? I have received this land from God alone, my land on which they have fortified themselves against my will. I have told them to retire from my land, but they build forts. Pere Rale, I come to you and ask that you write a letter to the great chief to the south, telling him of my declaration."

"I will write this letter for you, but it will increase hatred between the two nations. Are you ready to go to war again?"

Bomazeen spoke without hesitation. "I am."

"I will write the letter."

As stars rose over the village, Father Rale sat at his desk writing in the light of a bayberry candle. Wax dripped down the side; soon the flame would put itself out. He wrote the last line of the letter and put down his pen, knowing that he had just written his own death warrant. Tomorrow he would write a letter to his superiors in Quebec, telling him of Bomazeen's plan.

~~~~

Several weeks later, the letter was delivered to the British in grand style by one hundred chiefs and braves Father Rale and his superior, Father Pierre La Chasse. They were joined by an officer from Quebec. As Rale listened to the swish of paddles, he watched the French flag ripple in the breeze. Although France and England were officially at peace, this surprise visit would stir anger among the British officers. Colonel Henry Penhallow studied the scene with deep suspicion. Quickly he made his way down to the water and watched the canoes glide into shore. No greetings were exchanged. Chief Bomazeen handed him the letter. All the eastern tribes and their Canadian allies had signed the letter. It ended on an ominous note:

If the English do not quit our land in three weeks, we will burn your houses and kill your cattle.

Without response, Penhallow turned his back on Bomazeen and climbed a hill overlooking the harbor. He watched them paddle past small islands that dotted the bay. Hatred boiled up inside him; never had he felt so insulted. The Black Robe was behind all this, he fumed, stirring up revolt among the tribes.

He gave the letter to another officer. "Look at that writing. I am positive that the priest wrote it."

The officer studied the paper and nodded in agreement.

"I will bring it to Governor Dudley, and he will declare Sebastian Rale an outlaw. We will raid the village and kill the Black Robe. His scalp will bring a rich bounty." For Henry Penhallow, it was hard not to smile at the thought.

Chapter 18

Ambush

That is exactly what happened, much to the satisfaction of Penhallow. Soon Rale's scalp would be hanging in the public square as a warning to all other rebels who defy British sovereignty. Penhallow summoned two officers to his quarters. Captain Thomas Westbrook sat down in front of Penhallow, joined by another soldier. Westbrook's companion was a man with red, curly hair and yellow teeth that stuck out of his mouth. His name was Jeremiah Smith. Although still a young man, he was intelligent and strong, and thus was able to rise in the ranks quickly.

"Here is the official declaration by Governor Dudley, calling for the capture of the insurrectionist," Penhallow said, leaning back in his chair. It was a habit to fold his hands on an ever-widening belly and twiddle his thumbs. "Capture is a polite word. I think you know what I mean."

"We understand your orders, Colonel. Now we must decide when to strike," said Westbrook.

"I have given that matter much thought. Winter is the ideal time. When the rebels hear us coming and flee, we can easily follow their tracks in the snow. Rale has a bad leg, so he won't get far."

By January, snow was deep and the rivers frozen. It was also a time when the Wabanakis went to winter hunting grounds at the seashore. Mattawa, now a skilled hunter, joined other men of the village to fish and gather clams. He strapped on snowshoes and tramped through the forest. Despite biting cold, chickadees flitted among the pines. A snowshoe rabbit disappeared behind a rock. At that moment, Mattawa saw movement down by the river. British soldiers made their way up the riverbank, armed with rifles. In the blink of an eye, Mattawa snowshoed toward the village, skimming over the snow faster than he ever thought possible.

"Pere Rale! Pere Rale!" Mattawa shouted and burst into the priest's cabin without knocking.

Despite the cold, Mattawa's face was bright red and sweat beaded up on his forehead.

"What has happened?" the priest asked.

"I just saw English soldiers headed toward the village. They were carrying guns. You must hide!"

~~~~

In the winter it was painful process for Father Rale to walk at all. Arthritis settled into his bones, making every limb feel stiff. He threw on his cloak and glanced at his dictionary and strongbox but knew he could not carry them. He limped toward the church. Tabernacle keys jingled in his hand as a he fumbled to unlock the small door and remove the sacred vessels. He heard soldiers yelling, demanding to know of Father Rale's whereabouts.

Jeremiah Smith spoke sharply to his men. "Check the cabin. He must be hiding in there."

Quickly, Father Rale swallowed the consecrated Hosts, stuffed the sacred vessels into a box, and went out the side door into the forest. All the trees were stripped bare of leaves. It would be difficult to hide, but it was his only choice. Rale heard voices.

"He must have gone this way, down the path where the Indians get their wood. It is well-worn and easy for him to escape. Follow me," Smith said.

Father Rale hid behind a skinny birch tree, completely bare of leaves. He stared at the tree bark and tried not to breathe. Now the soldiers were marching straight at him, closer and closer. Finally, they were directly in front of the tree, eight steps away, so close that Rale saw the buckles on their boots. For some mysterious reason, they did not search behind the birch tree. They glanced left and right, behind rocks and over nearby hills, but without success.

"He slipped away," Smith ordered. "Let's check his cabin again."

With that order, they headed back to the village. As Rale waited for the soldiers to leave, he stood quietly behind the tree. He heard no gun shots, nor did he see smoke. On this occasion, the British were after him and did not burn down the village. Instead they left the village and headed south.

As he was unsure if the soldiers were still in the village, Father Rale hid behind the tree. His toes were numb with cold; every muscle was frozen like a block of ice. At long last, he heard footsteps crunch in the snow and the sound of breathing. It could be that the soldiers circled back to check again. A man called his name. It was Mattawa and he sounded worried, "Pere Rale, where are you? The soldiers are gone. It is safe."

"Over here," he answered weakly.

"I see you behind that tree."

"Help me. I cannot walk."

His frozen body fell like a tree chopped in the forest.

"I will run and get braves to carry you back."

Mattawa ran through the village shouting, "Pere Rale is hurt. He needs help!"

Gray Wolf emerged from his tent and Mattawa ran toward him, continuing to yell.

"Gray Wolf, you must go help," Shining Star said. He said nothing in reply, simply turned and left the wigwam.

Meanwhile, Father Rale lay in the snow clutching the sacred vessels and staring at the sky. It felt like the chalice had frozen to his body. Wisps of snow blew from evergreen boughs and landed softly on his face. Soon he felt the strong hands of Bomazeen try to lift him off the snow, but it proved impossible to do alone.

"We thought the soldiers would capture you. How did you escape?" the chief asked.

"I hid behind that tree."

Bomazeen glanced at the tree, "Impossible. The Great Spirit answered our prayers. I cannot carry you alone. I will get help from the village."

As Bomazeen stood up, he heard crunching of snow. Gray Wolf pushed aside evergreen boughs and knelt next to the priest.

"I will help," Gray Wolf said.

"You take his arms and I will hold his legs." Bomazeen said.

When they arrived back at Father Rale's cabin, they discovered that it had been ransacked. The writing table and chair were tipped over; his sleeping mat was thrown out into the snow and something was missing.

"Where is my dictionary ... and strongbox?" Father Rale asked.

Bomazeen scoured every inch of the cabin. "Gone."

Gone. The word stunned him. It felt like someone had stabbed him in the heart.

Chapter 19

Death Warrant

Captain Westbrook smoothed his hair and brushed lint from his uniform. At least when he gave the report on the mission to Norridgewock, he would look neat. He knocked on the door of Penhallow's office. Fortunately, Westbrook had something to show for his efforts. He tucked the large leather bag under his arm.

"Come in," Colonel Penhallow said. Westbrook sat down and paused in an effort to gather his thoughts.

"Well, what's the report?"

"He escaped."

Penhallow slammed his fist on the desk and roared, "Escaped? You fool, how could you let him slip through your fingers?"

"We searched everywhere … in the village …in the woods … behind rocks … he disappeared into thin air."

"You know he was there, and you could not see him?"

"Yes, sir."

"I ought to ship you off to the most desolate spot in the world, but I cannot."

"Why not, sir?"

"You are already there."

Westbrook opened the satchel. "Sir, I do have something to show for the mission."

"All I wanted was the Black Robe's scalp!"

"I know, sir, but I think you will be pleased."

He put the dictionary on Penhallow's desk. "This is the priest's dictionary of the Wabanaki language. It is 500 pages long and penned with impeccable precision. The loss of his life's work will be a crushing blow to the priest. He will know that we are close to capturing him. That will strike fear in his heart."

"I don't care about the book," he said and then pointed at the strongbox.

"What is that?"

"It is his strong box. I found this trinket." He dangled black rosary beads in front of the captain. "They use these to mumble prayers in what surely is a waste of time."

"Papists worship Mary. Those beads are instruments of the devil. Give them to me." With one yank, he pulled the rosary apart, causing the beads to spill on the table.

"Anything else? Any money?"

"Nothing."

Penhallow examined the box, revealing a secret drawer;

inside the drawer were letters, one written by Father Rale, the other by the governor of Quebec. "This could be significant. Have them translated and returned to me promptly. If this is what I think it is, we have proof that the Papist is inciting Indians to violence against us. Dismissed."

Westbrook stood at attention and saluted with vigor. As he left the office, Westbrook strutted out onto the cobblestone street. This letter could be all the evidence they needed to kill Rale and wipe out the entire village.

Chapter 20

Attack

On the morning of August 23rd, all was ready for the British attack on Norridgewock village. Captain Westbrook inspected his rifle one more time. Deep in his bones, he knew today would be a day of triumph. Today the scalp of Sebastian Rale would hang from his belt buckle. Two hundred soldiers stood waiting his command, joined by Captain Jeremiah Smith and Captain Johnson Harmon. They were joined by Mohawk Indians, allies of the British. Westbrook raised his arm and gestured toward the shore where seventeen whaleboats bobbed in the ocean. The plan was to row along the coast, leave the boats on a beach, and trek inland toward Norridgewock. The soldiers trotted to shore and climbed into the whaleboats. They rowed against ocean waves under a blistering hot sun. At times they were forced to carry their boats over small waterfalls until they reached the mouth of the Sebasticook River, where they set up camp. Westbrook summoned Jeremiah Smith.

"Captain Smith, I have heard that you are familiar with

paths leading through the forest toward Norridgewock. Is that true?"

"When I was a boy, the savages attacked our settlement and took me captive. An evil medicine man named Gray Wolf tried to make me his son. I fought against it with every fiber of my being," He stared at the dense forest. "Yes, I am familiar with these woods."

"I knew of this story. That is why I requested your presence in our maneuvers. I believe you must be motivated to eliminate the Indian threat to our settlements. The Black Robe stirs them up to attack us."

Jeremiah Smith tried not to show his eagerness to compete their mission. "What you say is true. I believe the best plan is to march inland and not upstream. Past the bend in the river are two large waterfalls and turbulent waters. I believe it to be impassable."

"Suggest a course of action."

"I know an old trail that cuts through the woods. It takes us to the village. It is thickly wooded, thus allowing us to sneak up on them undetected."

"Fine. That is what we will do. We will leave forty men behind to guard the boats and continue on foot."

All afternoon, the regiment hiked through the woods, hopeful that they would reach Norridgewock village by dusk.

Westbrook halted the men and listened. Far in the distance, he heard the sound of running water, sure to be the Kennebec River. Now the men moved quietly, certain that they would catch them by surprise. Little did they know that someone was watching.

It was Bomazeen. Still fleet of foot, the chief jumped over a log and ran to the village, desperate to arrive first to warn his people. Alert for any movement, Westbrook spotted him, and the race was on. At first, Bomazeen outdistanced the soldiers, leaping over rocks and dodging trees. Ahead lay a shallow spot in the river, swiftly flowing around a small island in mid-stream. Water splashed over his body as he made for the island. Quickly, he scanned the river to find a shallow spot. As he did, soldiers arrived at the riverbank. Smith raised his rifle to shoot. Westbrook pushed the musket down.

"No. This one is mine."

Westbrook raised his rifle and shot, hitting him in the back. Bomazeen fell into the stream, causing the clear water to run blood red.

~~~~

Meanwhile, Lily and Red Hawk did not know that the British were approaching. Danger seemed far away. To them, late summer was more than the month of the long sun; it was a time to watch shooting stars. Red Hawk patted Lily's black hair pulled back in a tight braid. "This is not a good night for watching stars. The moon is too bright. Look at the village below; it is bright as day."

"It makes me happy to be on this hill in the moonlight ... with you," she said.

"I am happy too," he said. "Perhaps the Great Spirit will send us a shooting star, like a heavenly visitor to show —"

Lily interrupted him. "I see one!"

Red Hawk squeezed her hand, "You are my shooting star, but do not be fleeting. Stay with me forever."

"I cannot imagine my life without you," she replied.

They hiked from the village to a hill off to the west where men had cleared a stand of oak for firewood. As they arrived at the crest, they saw the constellation Great Bear twinkling overhead. Down below, far away, was the village. On the edge of the cornfield, completely hidden in the woods, soldiers prepared for attack. Red Hawk and Lily still did not see them.

~~~~

Onward the soldiers marched under cover of thick woods until they reached a low range of hills that overlooked the village. By now the sun had set and they retired to their lodges. All appeared peaceful. Westbrook raised his spyglass and saw light shine from under the front door of Rale's cabin. Now all they needed to do was storm the village. Captain

Harmon edged over to the cornfields to prevent escape under cover of the towering stalks.

Captain Westbrook gave the order. "I will stay with part of the regiment back in the hills, prepared to ambush fleeing Indians. Smith, you lead one hundred men down the hill and make the initial attack. We have them surrounded."

Jeremiah replied crisply. "Yes sir."

Gray Wolf was first to spot the soldiers. He let out a war whoop. Men, women, and children ran out of their huts and were met with gunfire. As the British rushed out of the forest, bullets whistled past tree branches. Twigs and branches fell in their path. One of the first to die was an elderly man who fell in front of his wigwam. Blood dripped down from his chest.

Father Rale jumped up from his desk and opened the door. Smoke from the rifles filled the air. In a desperate attempt to rescue the sacred vessels, he limped toward the chapel. Jeremiah Smith pushed his way through the fleeing villagers, followed by three of his men, ever forward, toward the old priest. Suddenly, he spotted the priest limping toward the church. In order to get the perfect shot, Smith had to get closer. As he moved forward, leaders of the Wabanaki ran toward Father Rale, using their bodies to shield him from bullets. One of them was Gray Wolf.

"Fire!" Smith ordered.

Four men fell dead at their feet, directly in front of the tall cross planted in front of the church. Smoke from the rifles filled the air; bodies lay on the ground. The gray seal of death covered their faces and their lips curled in hard lines. Every inch of their clothing was soaked in blood.

"Fire!" Smith ordered again.

Three more villagers fell. Now Jeremiah Smith stood in front of the church, rifle loaded, ready to pull the trigger. The priest faced him without flinching. Jeremiah Smith closed his eyes and pulled the trigger. Father Sebastian Rale crumpled to the ground.

~~~~

Meanwhile up on the hill, Lily and Red Hawk heard the first crack of gunfire break the silence of a quiet night. In horror they watched redcoats swarm into the village, firing round after round. Gun smoke filled the air, women and children, old people screamed and ran for their lives. Over and over the soldiers fired their muskets. Red Hawk ripped away from Lily. He ran down the hill, but Lily was faster, overtaking him in a burst of speed like she had never known before. At the edge of a steep drop she sprang in front of him and thrust her body in his path. Tears streamed down her face, every feature was contorted, her face etched with grief lines. Her heart was breaking, bleeding with sorrow. She threw her arms around

Red Hawk and held onto him with all her strength.

Her throat burst with suppressed sobs. "Don't go ... I beg of you ... don't go! It is too late! We must survive."

They listened to gunfire until the deadly blasts stopped. Tears came, hot as fire. Terror took such hold of her that she felt dizzy and filled with nausea. She felt weak, as if all her bones had melted. Lily feared that all her family had died in the massacre. She was wrong. One lived.

~~~~

At the first boom of a gun, Mattawa knew they were under attack. Mattawa ran out of his cabin, yelling, "Run to the river! Follow me!"

With a child in his arms and old people struggling to keep up, Mattawa led the desperate flight to the river. He guided women and children into canoes and shoved the boats downstream. One after another he helped them climb aboard until there were no more boats. One soldier spotted them.

"Over here. More Indians! Shoot!"

Booming shots of guns split the air; Mattawa ducked as bullets flew over his head and with one flying leap he dove into the water. As he did, a bullet hit him in the arm. Blood spurt out from a deep gash in his arm. Mattawa went limp, pretending to be dead. It was his only hope. Now that the Kennebec River flowed bright red, the soldier turned back. He heard an order.

"Light torches. Burn the village."

And that is what they did, with zeal. In the middle of the village, soldiers lit pine torches that cast an orange tinge over the wigwams, cabins, and wooden chapel. With one touch of flame, the buildings were engulfed in a roaring inferno. It was complete destruction, complete except for one object. Father Sebastian Rale's cross, the cross that hung around his neck, did not burn. It was buried under soot and burning ashes in a place that later became a farmer's field.

Chapter 21

Mary Star-of-Night

Eight years passed since that tragic day. No longer was June simply the month when the Wabanakis hilled corn. Now in this year 1732, it was important to them as the month of Corpus Christi. Bright sun blessed the procession of people as they headed to the church, led by their priest, Father Jean LaChance, who held up the gold monstrance. The sky was clear and blue, with light fluted clouds drifting across it. Against the backdrop of sun and clear skies rose the Lord Jesus Himself, hidden in the consecrated bread, lifted up in a sparkling jeweled case.

Survivors of the Norridgewock massacre had fled to this place in Quebec, Canada. It was the village of St. Francis de Sales. One family trailed behind the procession. Red Hawk and Lily walked together, holding the hand of their seven-year-old daughter, Mary-Star-of-Night. Sunlight gleamed on her black hair — tied in braids that fell to her shoulders. She had a pretty, sweet face. Her eyes were clear as spring water and shone in dark brown colors, reflecting her joyful and gentle nature. As people entered the church, Red Hawk's family paused.

"Why are we stopping?" Mary asked.

Her mother smiled at the sound of her child's voice, fresh as the sound of a brook trickling over rocks. Lily said, "I have a surprise for you."

Mary saw her mother hiding something behind her back. "Close your eyes and hold out your hands."

Mary squeezed her eyes shut and eagerly awaited the gift. Lily placed something soft and round in her hands.

"Open your eyes."

It was a wreath filled with pink blossoms and pale green bayberries.

"Smell the flowers, Mary."

The little girl sniffed. "It smells like candles. Are these the berries Pere Rale used to make candles? You told me stories about him."

Lily nodded and placed the wreath on Mary's head. The smell of bayberries rubbed off on Lily's palms. She inhaled the fragrant scent. It brought her back to the day she watched Father Rale make his first candle. His face had lit up with delight, like a child on Christmas morning. For a moment, she felt so close to him, like he was there with her, seeing her happy family. A man came up behind them. It was Mattawa.

"Is that my Mary, Star-of-Night?"

He scooped her up with one arm, his only arm.

"Let me see …whose birthday is it today?"

She hugged Mattawa tightly around his neck. "It is mine."

"I have a present for you. It is a treasure I would give to only someone special like you."

Mary's eyes lit up with joy. Mattawa put the little girl down and reached into his leather satchel. He placed a wooden object in her tiny hands.

"What is it?" she asked

"I carved this many years ago for Pere Rale. He loved to slide it across the snow and play with us."

"I wish he would play with me." Mary turned the stick over in her hand. It was then that she noticed the crooked cross, carved those many years ago.

Mary stared at the gift, squinting in an effort to understand. "If I hug it, will Pere Rale pray for me?"

Red Hawk, Lily, and Mattawa did not answer, but only stared at each other. All of them sensed that a fourth person stood with them in spirit. The church bell rang, calling the faithful to prayer. Mary skipped along with her family, pressing the precious gift close to her heart.

Chiefs who died trying to protect Father Rale:

Bomazeen

Carabessett

Job

Mogg

Wissemet

Two more men of Norridgewock village died trying to shield Father Rale. An estimated 80 people were killed that day. There were 150 survivors, most of whom relocated to Quebec after the massacre.

End

Brave Hearts:
A Series Featuring
Catholic Heroes and Heroines

Perilous Days: Book One
A Classic Story of a Young Hero and his Dog

When a Nazi soldier knocks on the door of a quiet Catholic family, life is thrown into turmoil. Teenage son Felix becomes an unwilling soldier in the German army. The family also must protect their young son Willy, who has Down Syndrome and is danger of being targeted by Hitler's extermination plan. As Felix struggles to survive, he relies on his German Shepherd and a mysterious soldier who hides shocking secrets.

Awarded the Catholic Writer's Guild Seal of Approval!
Makes a perfect Confirmation gift.

About the Author

Born in Boston, Kathryn Griffin Swegart earned a master's degree from Boston College. She and her husband raised three children on a small farm in Maine.

Kathryn is the author of *Heavenly Hosts: Eucharistic Miracles for Kids* (second edition) which was awarded the Catholic Writer's Guild Seal of Approval and is an Amazon bestseller in Children's Christian Historical Fiction. She is also a professed member of the Secular Franciscans.